FOUR STEPS TO DEATH

S FOUR TEPS TO DEATH

DIANA RAMSAY

St. Martin's Press, New York

Design by Karin Batten

Library of Congress Cataloging-in-Publication Data

Ramsay, Diana.
    Four steps to death / Diana Ramsay.
        p. cm.
    ISBN 0–312–03835–6
    I. Title.
PR6068.A3349F68   1989
823'.914—dc20   89–27069

First Edition

10 9 8 7 6 5 4 3 2 1

For Tessa Sayle
with love and gratitude

FOUR STEPS TO DEATH

Chapter 1

Now that's really some-thing." A sallow-faced man in a bronze corduroy jacket was gawking at a pair of feet. On point, in fifth position, they appeared ready to bourrée across a stage. High arches and exquisite insteps were set off like jewels by a crisscross of pink ribbon; where the ribbon ended, so did the feet.

No, not a prop for the Grand Guignol. The feet, sculptured of pâté, were the pièce de résistance of a party buffet. An inside joke. Most of the guests knew the story of the Russian balletomanes who obtained a pair of Taglioni's slippers and served them up, cooked and garnished, at a banquet—and ate them, too.

"Must have taken a prodigious amount of work," said the man in the bronze jacket. "Seems a pity to eat it." He moved in on the pâté, gripping his plate purposefully.

Donnie Buell interposed, arm upraised like Rothbart, the evil genius of *Swan Lake,* forbidding Prince Siegfried to approach Odette. He made a rather pallid figure of menace in his dove gray silk shirt and smoky suede breeches; ever since his hair turned silver he has ostentatiously gone with it, even to the tint of his rimless glasses. All the same, the bronze jacket veered off to the mushroom pirogi.

Donnie stalked over to me and folded his arms across his chest. "Who's *that?*"

"No idea. Maybe a spy from *Gourmet* after your recipe." Donnie's pâté, which has a certain renown, contains Stilton, cream cheese, port wine, and he won't say what else.

"Hoo-hoo, Maggie. Very funny, I don't think." He scowled at me. "Where *is* the bitch anyway?"

"The bitch" was Nina Langlander, whose feet, the model for the pâté, had been photographed enough to be recognizable, most notably in a television commercial in which they performed chaînés around a heap of unset diamonds—a perfect juxtaposition, if you knew Nina.

"She'll be along. She's probably planning a spectacular entrance."

"Well, she'd better make it soon. I'm getting traffic warden's elbow holding off the ravening hordes."

"Relax. Nobody's in danger of starving for a while."

The big round table dominating the kitchen area of my living space was still crowded with *zakouski*, though the caviar was gone and great inroads had been made into the pirogi, the salads, the slices of black Russian rye spread with this, that, and the other. More to worry about in the drinks department. The number of guests was greater than anticipated, and champagne and chablis were flowing freely. Would the supply hold up?

I walked away from the table, distancing myself from these hostessy concerns. The premises might be mine, but Angela Cottman was throwing the party, in celebration of her daughter Phyllis's first solo at New York City Ballet. Ballet-struck at too late an age to make a career for herself, Angela had the heart and soul of a ballet mother, and the taste and restraint not to behave like one (at least most of the time).

A tiny, wrinkled face and a wispy white knot of hair caught my eye. Darya Akhsanova, Nina Langlander's ballet teacher, was enthroned in my rosewood armchair, with empty floor space around her wide as a moat. I went over to her and squatted at her feet, as Nina would have done. *"Bon soir, madame."*

"Bon soir, ma petite," she said uncertainly. She didn't recognize me, and I recalled Nina's telling me that Akhsanova was starting to show signs of her almost ninety years.

I smiled at her. "Can I get you anything, Madame?" Ritual patter. Her plate of *zakouski* looked untouched, and the flute glass perched on the arm of the chair was almost full.

She shook her head and pouted. "Where is she? Everything good will be gone if she does not come soon."

"I'm sure she'll be here as soon as she can, Madame."

"I hope so. You know how Maria Ivanova loves champagne."

It was all I could do to keep my smile intact. Maria Ivanova Korovskaya, my ballet teacher, had been Akhsanova's rival since St. Petersburg days, the two of them rarely losing an opportunity for backbiting. At parties, however, it was always armistice, with lots of embracing, guzzling champagne, and tearful reminiscing.

Korovskaya had been dead for nine years.

"Yes, I know how she loves champagne. I'll save a bottle for her."

"Dom Perignon?"

"Of course."

"Merci, ma petite."

I was spared having to keep it up by the arrival of the retired wardrobe mistress who lived with Akhsanova and looked after her. I excused myself and went in search of Phyllis Cottman to offer my congratulations. I spotted her in a huddle of young dancers who were as far as they could get from the goodies catered by Madame Arkadina (yes, really) and her niece Olga; I gave them high marks for willpower. In the huddle was Nina Langlander's daughter, Shelley Russell, angelic blond hair straggling out of its usually impeccable coil, an expression of sheer beatitude on her flawless face. Then I noticed the roach passing from hand to hand. That ticked me off. I've banned pot on the premises because the smell drifts down the stairs to my studio and many of my students are kids. But what's a taboo worth at party time?

"Do you want me to put a stop to that?" Anita Langlander, Nina's sister, materialized at my elbow in a teal blue smock dress that did a nice job of camouflaging the extra poundage she carried around. A coronet of rose-gold braids gave a touch of distinction to her round, placid face.

"Yes—no. What the hell, it's a celebration. Leave them alone. I'll spray in the morning if I have to."

"I'll keep an eye on them and see that things don't get out of hand."

Super-efficient Anita. Everything under control. She moved off to take up a sentry post near the youngsters before I had a chance to ask her what was keeping Nina. I moved off in the other direction and caught sight of the man in the bronze jacket again, getting an earful from Lydia O'Neill and looking dazed. Lydia, a pixie of a woman who once did a stint with Martha Graham and now teaches modern dance at Rutgers, has only two topics of conversation: macrobiotics and celibacy. I felt a twinge of pity for the guy.

"All right, everybody," Donnie shouted. "Come and devour the feet that sold a million diamonds!"

No second invitation was needed. There was a virtual stampede for the pâté, and great gobs were gouged out of it. Nothing like the reverent consumption the Russian balletomanes are said to have accorded the sacred relics of their idol. More like sharks in a feeding frenzy. The beautifully articulated feet collapsed into a mass of goo.

"Too bad Nina's missing this," Thea Davidson whispered in

my ear. Thea always whispers. She lost her voice permanently as a girl (bronchitis or some emotional trauma, the story goes), but you never think of her as handicapped. When Thea whispers, people listen.

"Yes. She would have wanted to be the first to taste. Well, too bad for her. She'll be lucky if Donnie doesn't skin her alive."

Thea raised her eyebrows, fiercely black against her pale skin. Her hair, black, too, with a patent leather sheen, was drawn back into a knot at the nape of her neck. Add long jet earrings, an onyx cigarette holder, the invariable mandarin collar (on ivory brocade lounging pajamas tonight), and you can see why, at the posh Greenwich Village school for girls she directs, they've tagged her "The Dragon Lady." Affectionately. Thea has a good heart. It's only her tongue that's dangerous—she's a relentless gossip.

"Aren't you even curious about where she could be?" Thea asked. "It isn't like her to be this late."

"No, it isn't." Nina was big on making entrances, but she had the heartiest contempt for holding-up-the-parade types ("They think they'll be more prized when they show. If only they knew"). Whatever was delaying her this long had to measure pretty high on the Richter scale.

"Should we be concerned, I wonder." Thea took a tranquil puff from the onyx holder. "Did I ever tell you about my niece's wedding? The groom didn't show up, and while we waited his reputation was carved to shreds. Later we found out he was in shreds, too. Collided with a semi on the way to the temple."

Before I had a chance to comment on that, Angela Cottman rushed up to embrace me, I could feel her breasts (38D) palpitate against my rib cage. "I'm so happy I could die. It's beyond my wildest expectations, seeing my own flesh and blood at the top of the tree. Well, not the *very* top, but a pretty high branch, wouldn't you say? Don't answer that. I don't want to hear it's only a beginning. I want to exult, I want to *gloat*. Oh my God, I remember how rebellious she was when she started. 'When I get big, Mommie, I'm going to make *you* do plié every day and see how *you* like it.' Then she got into it and never looked back. Oh my God, I'm so *proud* of her. Did you know when she started at SAB they thought she was borderline? Mr. B said—"

And she launched into a recital of every word George Balanchine was reputed to have uttered about Phyllis. Thea and I, careful not to look at each other, smiled, nodded, and clucked in the right places. We were both well schooled in the right places.

"Oh my God." Angela broke off in mid-spout, and her face clouded over. "I don't believe it. Couldn't he spare me tonight of all nights? Look at him!"

Stu Cottman paws a bit after he's had a few—a standard party turn and never any big deal. Tonight he had cornered my pianist, Mary Ann Sanders, and he had his arm around her and his lips practically glued to her ear.

I said I would handle it and started easing through the crowd toward them, wondering why, of all the women present, he had picked on Mary Ann, who worked hard at hiding her feminine lights under a bushel. The gray flannel suit she had on looked like something designed for your great-aunt Sarah, the one who believed clothes were meant solely to cover nakedness, as did her tailored white shirt and black brogues; her rimless glasses were firmly in place and her pale hair was anchored as usual in the tightest of pioneer woman knobs. On her face, an expression of martyrdom—anybody would have thought it was flames licking at her feet instead of poor harmless Stu licking at her ear.

"Aw come on, babe, loosen up," I heard Stu say. "I saw that look on your face, I know what it means. You were ready, don't try to tell me you weren't. So why the deep freeze all of a sudden?"

I used my elbows freely to close the gap. "There you are, Stu. I've cornered you at last." My voice throbbed with phony cheeriness and I didn't dare think about what my smile looked like, but somebody who thought he'd detected an amorous gleam in Mary Ann's eye had to be beyond sensitivity to nuances. I dislodged his arm from her shoulders and tucked it firmly under mine. "I want to powwow."

Stu blinked at me, totally bewildered, and who could blame him? But he said, "Sure," and flashed his endearingly lopsided grin. Nobody ever looked less like your typical lech than Stu, with his lanky frame, craggy patrician features, and general air of commitment to something all-consuming, like test tubes or terminals.

The captive, set free, glided away. Anybody else would have smiled at me or mouthed "Thanks." Not Mary Ann.

I apologized to Stu for barging in; told him I was thinking about making some high yield investments and wanted his advice. That sobered him up instantly, and he treated me to an analysis of current market trends that many a board room would have deemed it a privilege to hear. Wasted on me, of course. My head began to spin and it was all I could do to look attentive. When he slowed down, I thanked him, kissed him on the cheek, and made my getaway.

I made a routine check of the storage room next to the john and was heartened to find that the coats didn't have human company, either of the randy or the about-to-be-sick variety. Then I circulated and talked to a lot of people. Everybody seemed to be having a fine time. Glasses were filled to the brim and empty ones didn't stay empty very long. Including mine. The second time I went for a refill, I cautioned myself to go easy. The third time, there was a faint buzzing in my head and I resolved that this would be my last hit on the chablis. I fell in with the features editor of a suburban newspaper and got harangued on the deficiencies of dancers as directors of ballet companies, Mikhail Baryshnikov coming in for more than his share of vituperation. No sooner did I escape from him than I was cornered by a Soho jeweler who waxed rhapsodic on the Stuttgart Ballet. Pleading thirst, I went for another refill. I would pay for it in the morning, but what the hell.

I can't remember filling my glass again, which is not to say that I didn't. The buzzing in my head became a constant, but it wasn't painful. At some point I looked at the clock and was surprised to see that it was after ten. The evening had gone, but the people who call in at cocktail parties on their way somewhere else hadn't. That meant the wingding was a thumping success. I was glad for Angela's sake. I looked for her to tell her so, but she was hemmed in by well-wishers. Then I looked for Phyllis, but she and her little entourage of grass lovers weren't in evidence, and I deduced that they'd seized their opportunity to bug out and leave the scene as well as the food to the senior citizens.

Who else I saw and spoke to, what else happened, is a blur in my mind. Things became clear again in a hurry when Lydia O'Neill climbed up onto the table with the residue of the feast and proceeded to take off her dress—Isadora Duncan time. No matter how often you've seen an impression of Duncan, you always stop whatever you're doing to watch, never losing hope that somebody will make you see what she had that stood an entire generation on its ear. For me, nobody has come close, and poor Lydia was as far away as it's possible to get. In her white cotton knickers and camisole with no-nonsense grosgrain straps, scrawny arms fluttering one of my linen dish towels, she was a guaranteed downer. Sobriety settled over everybody like a pall. Embarrassment, too. The man in the bronze corduroy jacket, red in the face, went up to the table and pleaded with her. She paid no attention to him.

Thea Davidson shooed him away and took over. She began whispering to Lydia nonstop, jet earrings swaying with every syllable. Whatever she said worked. Lydia dropped the dish towel, jumped down from the table, landing in good demi-plié (once you learn how you never forget), and burst into tears. Thea embraced her and helped her into her dress without fuss. The two of them left, the bronze jacket right on their heels.

That was pretty much it. People started for the exit in droves. By and by everybody had left except for the diehards who would have to be pushed out. By me, probably, now that Thea, the world's greatest nonviolent bouncer, was gone. I suddenly felt exhausted, and very, very hot. I went into the kitchen area and leaned against the refrigerator. The coolness of the metal helped some. Not enough.

"Overdoing it, I see." Donnie Buell was at the sink, carefully washing the Georgian silver platter that had held the pâté.

"My problem."

"It certainly will be in the morning," he said, with disdain. Boozing brings out the Puritan in Donnie.

"Now, now." Angela Cottman swept to the sink, carrying two high stacks of plates. She set them down on the drainboard expertly (her father ran a trattoria for forty years). "Don't be a party poop."

"The party's over and she's pooped without any help from me."

"That I am. It was a great party, Angela."

"Yeah." Her face clouded. "Too bad Nina missed it. Funny. She said she was coming when I talked to her this morning."

"Maybe she eloped with a viscount," I said. "Or Sean Connery."

"I hope so," Donnie said venomously. "Then Robbie could track them down and save me the trouble of wringing her neck. The next time I do a life sculpture I'll choose somebody who'll show up to appreciate it. How about you, Angela? I could do your mammaries."

Angela laughed. "You'll be able to feed the world."

I started to laugh, too, but a wave of dizziness swept over me and the laugh turned into a moan. I leaned harder against the refrigerator so I wouldn't fall down.

Angela was all concern. "You ought to go up to bed, Maggie. We can tend to everything here."

"Don't be ridiculous. I'll be fine in a minute. Just let me catch my breath and—"

But Angela was at my side, her arm around my waist, steering me through the room. I rested my cheek against her head and closed my eyes, inhaling the heavy scent of Shalimar.

"Hope you make it," Donnie said loudly. "I'm not madly keen on mop-up detail."

I had just enough left to wonder how many people were still around to hear that, but not enough to raise my head and see. My feet negotiated the wrought-iron spiral staircase to my sleeping loft without a misstep. And then I was stretched out on my bed, head spinning, stomach churning.

"Nitey-nite." Angela tucked a blanket round me. "Don't let the bedbugs bite."

"They won't. Had the exterminator last week."

The last sound I heard was Angela's rich, throaty laugh. I sent up a little prayer that I wouldn't feel too awful in the morning and slid into oblivion.

Chapter 2

Sunlight streamed through the picture window of my studio, myriad specks of rainbow confetti in a shower of gold. A sight that greets me almost every fine morning, winter or summer. Starts the day right.

This day was all wrong. Nothing was going to put it right.

On the floor in front of me, Nina Langlander lay on her back, legs bent, arms outstretched. A steel skewer with a copper ring at the end protruded from her chest, and around it the gray silk of her dress was stained with blood.

When I dragged myself out of bed, my head had been throbbing. It was throbbing harder now. I wanted to step back through the door and come in again. Maybe Nina wouldn't be there second time round.

How idiotic can you get?

I walked over to the Steinway; set my mug of coffee down on the closed lid where mugs had been set too many times to count. Somehow things should have been different this time. The mug should have overflowed, exploded, done something. But it just stayed there.

I looked around the studio. Surely I would see everything askew, tainted by the horror on the floor. But all was as usual, including the involuntary stirring of pride deep inside me. It's a dream studio, very large, spanning the width of the building and most of the length, with a high ceiling and a floor of handpicked pine boards. Two of the walls are practically all window from chest level on up, with barres underneath. The third wall has the mirror, treated twice a week with vinegar water, and in front of it the Steinway. The fourth wall has the door and a long, backless bench for visitors (not mothers. Ever). Maybe the place isn't the wonder of the Western world, but I'm forever besieged with requests to rent it out for classes, rehearsals, even recitals. I always refuse. I can't bear the thought of anybody else taking over my studio, even temporarily.

Now it had been taken over with a vengeance.

I wanted to go on denying. Do my customary early morning tour of inspection. Test the floorboards. Tug at the barres to make sure gremlins hadn't loosened them in the night.

Time to face reality. Nina was lying in the middle of the floor. Dead. She had to be dead. She could never be so still for so long if she were playing some bitchy practical joke, if in a minute she would pick herself up off the floor and say, "Ketchup. Fooled you, didn't I?" and laugh her head off.

Could she?

Nothing for it. I had to find out for sure.

I discovered that my palm was stuck to the lid of the piano—I hadn't even been aware I was leaning. There was a sucking noise as I pulled free.

Up close, the first thing that registered was Nina's eyes. They were wide open, the irises like disks of lapis lazuli, looking straight up at me. No, not *at* me—through me. Her upper lip was lifted in the start of a snarl. Or something else. I bent over to touch her cheek, but the sightless stare held me off like a laser ray. I had to straighten up and back off. What I couldn't find out by looking, I wasn't going to know.

I looked. At the magnificent russet hair, fanned out around her head as if arranged for one of those classy-erotic lingerie ads. At the open karakul coat, the blood on the smoky silk shirtwaist dress, the curve of her bare throat.

No, that was all wrong. She should have been wearing a necklace. Pearls or amethysts or one of her antique silver chains. I looked at her hands. The baroque pearl ring she always wore was gone. So was her watch.

A mugging, obviously. Somebody had sneaked in here during the party last night and robbed and killed Nina. The kind of thing you read about every day, and a part of your mind thinks "There but for the grace of God" and distances it as fast as possible. Only I couldn't distance this.

I couldn't quite believe it either. Why would a mugger kill her? Nina loved jewelry passionately, but she loved life more. She would have given up every trinket she had on without hesitation. From the look of the body, there hadn't been any struggle. A sadistic junkie, perhaps?

It still didn't compute. Why?

The skewer. I knew it had an angled point, just as I knew it had to be rubbed with steel wool every couple of months so it wouldn't blacken. Back when Bloomingdale's brought off a trade coup with mainland China and stuff from there began to flood the market, I had bought a dozen just like it. They were upstairs on my kitchen counter, in a fifty-year-old Chianti bottle.

Not all twelve, I was suddenly sure.

The tumult in my head shot through the rest of me. I backed away from Nina and lowered myself into a squatting position. Too fast—a red-hot clamp closed over my left knee. I massaged the kneecap with my fingers. As if that would help. As if anything could.

Assuming it was one of my skewers, anybody at the party could have taken it and gone downstairs to wait for Nina. How many suspects? Sixty? Seventy? Well, that certainly left the field wide open.

And what was to say the murderer hadn't pinched the skewer in advance, hidden in here, done his dirty work, and gone home without appearing at the party at all? Not the likeliest of possibilities, but not to be discounted entirely. Anybody could walk into the building while I was teaching a class and make off with anything he could carry, as I knew only too well—I'd been robbed three times.

It wasn't a theory the police were likely to be crazy about. No doubt they would concentrate on the people at the party.

Especially me.

Backing off was mental this time. I looked round the studio again. Caught sight of my mirror self in an ocean of space, hunched like a cornered animal. Not a very edifying spectacle. I wrenched my eyes away, careful not to let them seek out Nina. They lighted on a hand-knitted leg warmer lying on the floor under the visitors' bench, a potpourri of blues and purples, cables and lattices and bobbles. Clearly some devoted mother had labored hard. Would she throw a fit over the loss? Probably, and then set to work on a replacement. What was the thing doing here anyway? I never let my students wear leg warmers—they hide too much.

My mind was playing Trivial Pursuit. Small wonder. Sixty or seventy suspects with opportunity to kill Nina, but whose so good as mine? That was what the police would think. And when they started hunting for motives, they would find a slew of them, Nina being Nina, but the minute they came up with mine I was willing to bet I would be the Abou Ben Adhem of their suspect list. Never mine that Nina and I had buried the hatchet ages ago.

The cornered animal started to shiver. I gripped my upper

arms tightly till the fit subsided. I couldn't afford to give way. I had to get myself up the stairs and call the police, just as any innocent person would do. Damn it, I *was* an innocent person.

I kept my eyes on the leg warmer. Neutral object. Maybe the trivia would crowd in again, calm me down. Leg warmers. Legs. Feet. Nina's feet, molded of pâté. Donnie standing guard over them, waiting in vain for the one reaction that mattered, and then the wooden spatulas gouging, gouging, gouging. Tears welled up and started to flow, and in a moment I was sobbing uncontrollably. I didn't know whether I was crying for Nina or for Donnie or for myself.

The flood subsided. I got up, took a last look at Nina, and went to check out the dressing room, pulling aside the curtain that shields the modesty of my token male students, opening the door of the john. God knows why. The killer wasn't likely to have spent the night. I suppose I thought there might be signs that somebody had holed up to wait. I didn't see any.

The police dispatcher was efficient—I didn't have to repeat a thing. When I hung up the phone, I counted the copper rings fanning out of the top of the Chianti bottle. Eleven skewers. For a wild instant I considered telling the police that I had lost the twelfth long ago. But what if there were tests that could prove the murder weapon had been in close proximity to the skewers in the bottle? The truth was safer.

Christ, I was thinking like a criminal. What ever happened to innocent till proven guilty?

I telephoned Mary Ann Sanders to tell her I wouldn't need her till Monday. There was empty air on the line as she waited for the explanation that common courtesy required, but I wasn't up to it and said I would get back to her. Then I telephoned Monique Goldman, a former student who runs an answering service, and asked her to get out the list of my Saturday students and let them know classes were cancelled. I didn't offer her an explanation either, and, though she must have longed to ask, she didn't.

Well, she would know soon enough. So would Mary Ann. So would everybody.

I had to hunt for my front door CLASSES CANCELLED sign, and was just digging it out from under a stack of place mats when the doorbell rang. Perfect timing. The two patrolmen on my doorstep looked like teenagers (proof that I've really hit middle age, as if I need it), but they knew their job. They took the sign out of my hands and hung it on the door, then followed me up to the studio without stomping or dragging their feet; looked at Nina as if she were a museum exhibit; touched her to be sure she wasn't. One of them went back outside, presumably to radio in a report. The other took me through the story of how I found Nina and said it must have been a great shock, and wouldn't I be more comfortable waiting upstairs until the officer in charge arrived. Probably a meaningless civility (he was between me and a getaway, wasn't he?), but I was grateful for it anyway. I managed not to race up the stairs.

I sat down at the kitchen table and fell into a stupor until sounds of activity wafted up the stairwell. I visualized hordes of solid blue bodies tramping around my studio, a place where flesh was supposed to take wing and soar. Resentment surged up in me at the intrusion on my private space, and I had to fight down an impulse to run down and shout that I wanted everybody to clear out. Shock must have disordered my priorities. Or maybe that's being too charitable.

I spread my hands over the table and pressed until my fingers could feel the grain of the wood. As solid as a prop could be. The table is a circular slab of walnut a foot thick and eight feet in diameter set on an oval ebony pedestal, the work of a sculptor from Carmel who passed through my life briefly. Around it are half a dozen hickory spoke-back armchairs I spotted on the veranda of a farmhouse in Maine from the window of a bus. They're at least a hundred years old and very crudely carved, but somehow they work with the table and with a living space as open and ample and nearly as uncluttered as the studio downstairs.

"No frills nitty-gritty," Nina had remarked the first time she visited me here. "Reminds me of West 111th Street." The reference was to the apartment we had shared during our last two years of college, a smallish two and a half with a living room bare except for a barre, a big wall mirror, and giant pillows (many a time I had to sack out on those pillows because Nina had overnight company). I had no problem calling the place home, but for Nina it was a campsite. She was into amassing things. Clothes. Furs. Jewels. Antique furniture. Men. More and more as the years went by. Compensation, the amateur psychologist might say. Once upon a time Nina had aspired to be another Danilova, all brio and diamanté twinkle and star presence.

My eyes misted over. Once again I wasn't sure exactly what I was crying for.

I heard footsteps coming up the stairs and hastily wiped my eyes. They were heavy footsteps, the footsteps of somebody who didn't mind throwing his weight around. There was a perfunctory rap on the open door, and a man came in. He looked like a weight thrower. Tall and broad across the shoulders and maybe other places as well, a loosely belted olive drab trenchcoat making it hard to tell. No-nonsense face, fleshy but not flabby, with a beak of a nose, jutting cheekbones and chin, hooded dark eyes that probably played possum a lot. Ruddy bronze skin and straight black hair worn a little too long gave him a vaguely Indian appearance.

He stopped and scrutinized me for what seemed an excessive length of time, then stalked up to the table. "Detective Sergeant Tagliaferro. Homicide."

I stood up to examine the ID he held out. If he was the slightest bit disconcerted to find my chin nearly on a level with his (men his size aren't used to that), he didn't show it. No doubt he was Godfather of his tribe and merry hell on the warpath. His first name was Anthony. Of course. What else would it be?

"I'm Maggie Tremayne."

"So I gather." The hooded eyes took my measure again,

surveyed my living space warily, as if he expected something nasty to pop out of the woodwork, returned to me with a speculative look that made me wonder if he thought the nasty something was me.

Maybe I was reading him wrong. When you're part of the ballet scene, people either overdo the adulation or behave as if they've met a citizen of Gomorrah; there doesn't seem to be anything in between.

"That CLASSES CANCELLED sign of yours looks pretty well worn. You must cancel a lot."

"Three times in fourteen years. It got rained on during a storm."

"You don't say." A slight curl of his upper lip. Maybe he was the kind who thought dancers were made of glass. Or maybe he was just a supermacho pig.

I found myself hoping he had a wife who got on him about his weight.

The speculative look came into his eyes again, and he switched gears. Suggested we both sit down. Asked me, almost politely, to tell him about finding the body. I did. He asked me if I had any ideas about how it happened. I told him about the party Nina hadn't turned up for and how I assumed from the way she was dressed that she had been attacked on her way in. Naturally he wanted to know everything I could remember about the party. Nothing showed on his face as he listened, not even when he heard the size of the guest list—I had to give him points for that. He didn't take notes, but I was sure he didn't miss anything.

When I finished, he thanked me and said I had been very concise. "A couple of things puzzle me, though. Why didn't Mrs. Cottman throw the party at her own house? Why here?"

"She lives in Englewood. That's too far to go for a cocktail party if you happen to have a dinner engagement or an evening performance to attend. Then, too, for many of the people she invited the suburbs are out of bounds. You see, Angela got hooked on ballet when it was still dominated by the old Russian guard, and the survivors of that era tend not to be able to go far from home or not to want to. Everybody can get here. And my living space can accommodate a lot of people."

"I can see that. The other thing that bothers me is why you left your studio door open. Seems to me that with all those people trooping in and out of the building you'd want to lock up."

"No, I wouldn't. I always leave the studio door open. Wide open. Dancers work hard and they sweat a lot. If the stale air gets trapped inside the studio overnight—"

"I get the picture. Okay. Everybody knows about the open studio, so it would have been relatively easy for somebody to wait for Ms. Langlander and ambush her on her way up to the party. Can you remember any of the guests behaving peculiarly? Somebody having a higher high than usual? Somebody acting nervous?"

"Not really. It was a party, after all. And for a lot of the people who came, peculiar behavior is a way of life."

"Fair enough." The corners of his mouth twitched slightly. "I presume that you left the outside door unlocked for the duration of the party because it was too much trouble to hit the buzzer every time the doorbell rang. Right?"

"Yes. There's safety in numbers."

"Sure. If you live in a cozy little village where your big problem is the local rowdies tanking up and trying to crash the gate. But let's not get into that. What time did you unlock the door for the first guest?"

"I . . . Actually, it wasn't quite like that. As a rule I lock up after my last class ends at five, but yesterday people were bringing over food and—" The look in his eyes paralyzed my vocal cords.

"So you're telling me just about anybody could have walked in off the street from five o'clock on to ambush Nina Langlander. Including our old friend the junkie burglar who panicked when she threatened to yell. Is that what you're telling me?"

"I wouldn't presume to tell you anything, Sergeant Tagliaferro.

Naturally I thought of a burglar right off. There wasn't any jewelry on the—Nina loved jewelry. She would have worn a necklace with that dress. And she always wore a baroque pearl ring. Not to mention that she would as soon have gone out of the house naked as without a watch. But . . . Well, removing the jewelry might have been a ploy to make it look like an outside job."

"'Outside job?' 'Ploy?' Interesting terminology, Ms. Tremayne."

"You can spare me the irony. Whoever killed Nina probably used one of my skewers. It matches the others in the bottle on the kitchen counter, in case that little detail has escaped your notice."

"When did you discover a skewer was missing?"

"Right after I telephoned you. There were a dozen the last time I rubbed them down. That was weeks ago. I haven't touched them since."

"I see." His stare was level and passionless; I felt as if I were being appraised by a calculator. "I'm still wondering about your choice of the word 'ploy.' For the sake of argument, let's suppose that somebody who knows all about Ms. Langlander's penchant for jewelry finds himself a little short, puts a stocking over his head, watches at the window for her to arrive, and tries to rob her. In spite of the stocking she recognizes him and shows that she does and he feels he has to kill her. It plays, doesn't it?"

"Well, yes, I suppose so. Anything's possible, but—"

"But you're reluctant to accept it. Why? Because you balk at the idea of robbery among friends? Or because you can think of a better motive for Ms. Langlander's death?"

That one left me thrashing on the line. He didn't reel in, though. He said he had things to attend to downstairs and would be back shortly. In the meantime, would I mind compiling a list of as many of the party guests as I could remember? I said I wouldn't mind.

He left. I collected a pad and pencil, my address book from the shelf under the wall phone, my stack of telephone directories from the storage room, and buckled down to work. I was glad to have something to do, even if it was tedious. Maybe because it was tedious.

There were a couple of interruptions. A young detective with a white-blond crew cut that showed a lot of pink scalp came up to ask if he might "borrow" my skewers "for the lab." I almost had to bite my tongue to refrain from telling him he was welcome to keep them. He picked them up with tongs, dropped them into a plastic bag, thanked me, and left. Then came a gray little man with what looked like a stamp pad to take my fingerprints ("Just a formality, ma'am. Don't worry, it washes right off"), and after he left I scrubbed my fingertips long and hard, way past the point of necessity, feeling a little like Lady Macbeth.

Nonetheless, I was finished with the list by the time Sergeant Tagliaferro paid me the promised return visit. He raised his eyebrows when he looked it over.

"You didn't exaggerate the head count, did you?"

"I can't pretend it's comprehensive. There were plenty of strange faces. There always are at parties like this, when people feel free to bring their friends along. You can easily fill in the blanks by asking around."

"I'll make a note of that." His tone was bland, yet he managed to make me feel like an idiot.

"I'm sure."

He ignored the sarcasm. "About the people on the list. I gather from what you said earlier that Mrs. Cottman goes way back with most of them. Including Ms. Langlander?"

"Yes. The dance world is pretty inbred."

"I suppose you go way back with Ms. Langlander, too? Bought your first pair of toe shoes together and all that?"

"Actually, no. We met in college."

"College?" He made no attempt to hide his surprise. "I didn't think dancers went to college. No offense intended."

"None taken. You're quite right. The college years are prime dancing time and most ballet dancers feel they can't afford to spend big chunks of it in the classroom. I come from an academic family, though—my father taught mathematics at NYU—and not going to college was sort of unthinkable. Maybe an offer I couldn't refuse would have turned me around, but nobody made me one. Nina's situation was different. She got into the New York City Ballet at fifteen, but after a couple of years there she was convinced she wasn't going to make it big and quit. Decided she wanted to run an art gallery instead, so college was in order. Nothing came of that ambition, of course. Dancing was in her blood. As you may know, she had quite a decent career on Broadway, and for a few years she and I were members of a quartet that satirized classical and not-so-classical ballet. The *Pas de Quatre*. Does that cover the ground, Sergeant Tagliaferro?"

"Admirably. Thanks, Ms. Tremayne. You've been a great help." He got to his feet. "We'll be packing up in a few minutes. You'll hear us. When you do, you can go down and bolt the door."

"Are you going to put a seal on the studio or anything like that?"

"No. We've done our work and you have a business to run." As he went out the door, he said, "I'll be in touch." He didn't add, "Don't leave town" or any euphemism for it. But then he didn't have to, did he?

He was as good as his word. About ten minutes later, I heard the unmistakable sounds of departure. His troops didn't make a whole lot of noise going down the stairs, but it shook me up anyway. How could it fail to? I knew they had to be carrying Nina.

The front door closed. Obeying instructions, I went down to lock and bolt it. Hurrying, as if there were reason to hurry. Passing the studio door without a glance inside. I made a big bang shooting the bolt home, in case anybody was lurking outside to check up on me.

Starting up the stairs, I told myself that now I had to walk into the studio, reestablish that it was my studio, no matter what.

I stopped halfway to the landing. Could I face it? Nina's body might be gone, but what about the chalk outline television police shows are so fond of? Most likely Tagliaferro would have had it removed. Still, with or without the *aide-mémoire*, I wouldn't be able to look at my studio floor without seeing Nina lying there.

My studio floor. That had to make me the leading suspect.

But Tagliaferro had let me off the hook. How much comfort could I take in that? Very little. He was bound to be back after he tapped the grapevine. People would fall all over themselves to tell him why Nina and I had been at odds for years. Lots of people. Next time he would have a really sharp hook and there wasn't a chance I would be let off. He would jerk me around every which way. Watch me wriggle. *Enjoy* it.

Maybe I was going overboard.

Maybe I wasn't.

I continued on up to the landing. Stopped outside the studio door. Went past it without a glance inside. Gutless.

The kitchen clock said twenty past twelve. Incredible, so much happening in so short a space of time. Eight o'clock, when I went downstairs for my ritual morning inspection, seemed like a couple of weeks ago. Now practically the whole day lay ahead of me. What the hell was I going to do with it?

I'm not a workaholic, and as a rule I glory in my leisure time. But cataclysm shatters all the rules. I couldn't resort to my usual quick fixes for disaster—a visit to the Dance Collection at Lincoln Center Library, a window crawl of Columbus Avenue, shopping at Zabar's—for fear of running into people who had heard about Nina and would want all the lurid details. The media wouldn't be firing their first shots yet, but Tagliaferro's myrmidons were probably tackling the party guests right this minute. The dance world is small. News travels through it like a whirlwind. Walls, closed doors, sealed lips are no impediment. Especially not sealed lips.

My telephone started ringing. I let it ring. I'm not wild about talking on the telephone at the best of times, and I don't have an answering machine. If people want to talk to me when I'm in the mood to talk, fine. If not, let them talk to somebody else.

Since I couldn't face going out, my back-up plan was a stiff workout followed by a long, hot bath. I unrolled a floor mat in the middle of my living space, put Mozart's *Les Petits Riens* on the stereo, and performed an up-tempo sequence of stretching exercises. It wasn't a patch on a proper barre, but by the time the record ended I was nice and loose. I rolled up the mat, changed the record for the adagio of the Mendelssohn Scotch Symphony, and performed a slow, tortuous adagio of my own. For a finale, some presto combinations to the closing rondo of the Beethoven First Symphony. Terre à terre combinations, every one. No jumps for me. Ever. By the time I was through, the sweat was pouring off me.

I went into the bathroom and turned on the bathtub taps full force, came out to quench the thirst I'd worked up with water and lemon juice, sipping slowly. The tub was almost full when I returned to the bathroom, and I realized I'd forgotten to put in bath salts. Too late now. I stripped, untaped my left knee, turned off the taps, and climbed into the tub. "Climbed" is no exaggeration—my bathtub is a big old eyesore complete with claw feet, very high and very deep. I can submerge like a submarine if I want to; I've even tried snorkeling through a straw. Now I sat ramrod stiff, my back supported by the almost perpendicular wall of the tub, my legs stretched straight out ahead of me.

I closed my eyes. And said to myself: Nina's dead. Nothing happened. My thought processes failed to stir. No flood of feeling surged in my breast.

The steaming water induced a pleasant lassitude, and I let myself become a vegetable. Almost. Part of my brain kept track of time. Going noddy-nod in the tub and coming to when the water has gone cold is a real bummer. I picked up the soap, and all of a sudden an image came into my head: Nina in a pale mauve tutu with a satin bodice, a fat red sausage curl on each side of her

Psyche knot, bourréeing across the stage with her arms framing her head, glancing flirtatiously back over her shoulder. The image was from a pas de deux she and I had performed often, a parody of Fanny Elssler and her sister Therese, who specialized in cavalier roles because she was tall (Auguste Bournonville said she always appeared as if she had just fallen from the clouds). The number had been one of the *Pas de Quatre*'s greatest hits.

The soap slipped out of my hand and into the water with a plop. I groped for it blindly. My eyes were full of tears. I gave up on the soap and just sat there and let the tears fall. No racking sobs. No constriction in the throat. Just the waterworks, flowing and flowing and flowing.

Strenuous ringing of my doorbell snapped me out of it. Somebody who hadn't been able to rouse me on the phone, most likely.

"Go away!" I shouted with every bit of lung power I could commandeer.

The pounding stopped.

"Go away!" For good measure.

Silence. My would-be visitor was gone. I retrieved the soap and buckled down to the job of scrubbing. I was altogether myself again.

I discovered I was ravenous. As soon as I was out of the tub and into my terrycloth burnoose, I made a beeline for the refrigerator and gorged on the party food Angela had left for me—tongue with horseradish sauce, stuffed tomatoes, mushroom caviar, pirogi. Everything tasted wonderful.

Chapter 3

The first time the phone rang I didn't answer. Whoever it was would think I was still in bed, a legitimate place to be at ten past seven on a Sunday morning. Actually, I was up and taping my left knee, as I do first thing every morning, as I'll probably have to go on doing first thing every morning for the rest of my days. By now I can do the taping blindfold. First I wind a strip of two-inch linen tape around my thigh eight inches above the knee and another strip around the middle of my calf. Loosely—movement is the name of the game. Then I tape *x*'s on both sides of the knee from strip to strip, alternating and overlapping; I leave the kneecap free and frame it with a little hem of tape. Finally I wind three-inch elastic tape around my leg to cover up the linen tape, and voilà! If mummification ever makes a comeback, I'll be ready.

The second time the phone rang, I was brushing my hair. Again I didn't answer. The doorbell, however, was another matter. It rang as I was finishing my wake-up coffee, and I felt I couldn't ignore it. What if it was an emissary from Sergeant Tagliaferro? Flak on that front was the last thing I needed. I went downstairs and asked who it was before I put a hand near the bolt.

"Such prudence, darling," Donnie Buell answered. "I thoroughly approve."

I opened up, and Donnie came in, carrying a teapot wrapped in a Morris print cozy. He grazed my cheek with his lips. "I couldn't rouse you by phone so I decided to see what flesh and blood could do."

"Reckless of you. What if I'd decided not to answer the door? You would have wasted your brew."

"You needn't remind me. Yesterday evening I made the most divine syllabub and brought it round and got shouted off like a mongrel. I had to drink it all by myself. I must look a wreck." Donnie swept past me and marched up the stairs like visiting royalty, the pale gray muffler wrapped around his throat lacking only a few feet of doing duty as a train. He went past the studio without a glance inside and continued on up to my living space. Waving me imperiously to a chair, he set the teapot down on the table and relegated my coffee mug to the sink. He opened a cupboard and got out two bone china cups and saucers and brought them to the table.

"Make yourself at home, why don't you."

"Don't be tiresome, love." Donnie sat down, unwound his muffler, and unzipped his silver suede jacket; around his neck was a hammered silver crucifix almost large enough to hang on the wall. "I was in Philadelphia yesterday, and the minute I got home what do I find on my doorstep? Fuzz. That's how I heard about Nina."

"Not a good way."

"No." He poured out the tea, which had a particularly acrid smell. "They grilled me to a turn about the party. The shock didn't really hit me till after they left. Then I make the syllabub and rush over here to share it with you and what do I get? Rejection."

"Umm." I took a sip of tea. Not only did it taste as foul as it smelled, it prickled going down—the kind of prickling that makes you wonder if hair will sprout where it passes.

"That's right, love, drink up. I call it Devastation Be Damned. I whipped it up for Jerry Harding when that little tart walked out on him and it made him mind ever so much less."

I could believe that. Drink enough of this stuff and you might well be beyond minding anything. I watched Donnie as he sipped, slowly and meditatively, holding the cup below his chin with both hands, like a chalice. All at once, the lines of care and wear in his face were smoothed out, the smooth cap of silver hair was transformed to gold, and I was wrenched back in time . . .

"You bourrée across front stage left to backstage right, Nina. The audience will see your tiny-minded concentration in the set of your shoulders and laugh their heads off. Guaranteed." Donnie smiled impishly over the rim of his cup.

"Terrific," said Nina. "And just how am I supposed to pop up front stage left? On a wire? Like Peter Pan?"

"Nothing as crude as that," said Terry Sablier. "You come out of the orchestra pit. The troops lift you up and over. It probably wouldn't do any harm if you wobble a bit and veer off course far enough to bowl Maggie over. Literally."

"Thanks," I said. "But you might have a problem with Local 802 if you ask the musicians to pick up anything but their instruments."

"They won't complain," Nina said. "Not when they'll be getting the chance to cop a feel."

Terry threw back his head and roared. It always came as a surprise, that full-throated laughter of his. Tall and gangly, with fine straight dusty blond hair and pale blue eyes that peered nearsightedly and shyly out of your quintessential woeful counte-

nance, he looked like a Hollywood version of a classical musician.
Which proves they don't always get things wrong . . .

I pulled out of memory lane. Terry was dead. Nina was dead.
I forced myself to tune in on what Donnie was saying.

"—ironic that somebody should kill her now. A year ago, even
six months ago, I could see. Our Nina traditionally took a certain
amount of pride in making a running for Bitch of the Year. But
lately she'd been positively anemic in tooth and claw. Those oil
wells were the be-all and end-all—one couldn't even converse
with her anymore. Of course she might have bored somebody to
utter desperation, but one has to go with the obvious. It must
have been some street crazy after a score."

"I fail to see that one has to go with anything. It's the police
who have to worry about hypothesizing. Anyway, people have
been known to hold grudges for years and years."

"True, darling, but with Nina one was tempted to scratch her
eyes out on the spot. Not six months later. Not even six minutes
later. Of course I'm not saying she was chosen entirely at
random." He took a dainty sip from his cup, his eyes, the color
of wet stones, contemplating me levelly. "I was thinking along
the lines of somebody meeting the sort of person a somebody
would be a lot better off not meeting. But unfortunately the
realization comes too late—there's that foot in the door."

"Not Nina."

"Actually, I wasn't thinking of Nina." Silver lids dropped like
shades. "It's your house, Maggie love. Made any friends lately
who turned out to be greedy whackos?"

"Not lately."

The shades snapped up, and he flashed me a disarming grin.
"Nice of you to refrain from pointing out that it's more or less the
pot calling the kettle black." Donnie has a predilection for leather
bars that even the AIDS hysteria has failed to curb.

"The kettle isn't all that spotless. I suppose I should be glad
you're opting for a crazy instead of me."

"*You?* What an absurd idea."

"I doubt that the police think it's absurd." I almost blurted out that it was almost certainly my skewer that had killed Nina, but I restrained myself.

"They don't know you. As a suspect, you simply don't cut it. I can see you throttling Nina with your bare hands or bashing her over the head with your stick in the heat of the moment. But sneaking up on her and stabbing her and taking her jewelry as a blind? No way."

"Should I thank you for that? Or what?"

"We'll take gratitude as read." Donnie poured himself more herbal tea. It was the color you see in pools of stagnant water with unimaginable things breeding in their depths. "Buck up, Maggie love. It doesn't have to be *your* crazy. It could be anybody's crazy."

"How comforting."

"If I were you I'd make steady use of the bolt on the outside door for a while. Whoever stabbed Nina could easily decide there might be more pickings here and—"

The doorbell cut him off. A quick ring, then a carillon of sound as somebody pressed a finger to the button and left it there.

"Oh God." Donnie clapped his hands over his ears. "Buzz back. Quick. Never mind about security. So much bluster can't possibly be a real threat."

I got up to press the buzzer. The ringing stopped. The front door slammed and footsteps pounded up the stairs, across the landing, up the second flight. Milton Frankovich, the dermatologist who leases the ground floor of the building for his office, rushed in.

"I just heard!" Horrified, but with an undertone of grievance, as if he felt he had a right to know sooner. "I tried to telephone you, Maggie, but I couldn't get an answer. I was listening to the news while I was shaving. I almost cut my throat."

"Almost doesn't count," Donnie purred. "Of course you weren't at the party, so the police wouldn't want to talk to *you.*" He made it sound like being excluded from the Russian Tea Room.

Milton, a balletomane committed to the belief that tolerance for gay bitchery goes with the territory, produced a weak smile, ghastly with the look of profound sorrow in his slightly drooping dark brown eyes (the kind usually described as soulful). "Poor Nina. She was a fine woman. In every sense."

"*Every* sense?" A postprandial barracuda smile lit up Donnie's face. "That sounds suspiciously like intimacy. Surely our Nina was a bit long in the tooth for you."

This was a dig at Milton's well-known predilection for young dancers, and it drew blood—all the way up to Milton's face. "We were never intimate in that sense."

Which, I happened to know, was an out-and-out lie. Nina had told me about the time she barged past Milton's receptionist and waiting patients into his office, peeled off her clothes, and offered him a choice between calling for help and locking the door; he had locked the door. Though he had been all for a return bout, Nina had passed ("Patticakes with the romper brigade is about his speed").

Donnie raised a quizzical eyebrow. "Methinks the gentleman doth protest too much," he said, so mildly that I was sure Nina hadn't told him about that day at the office.

Milton, however, drew the opposite conclusion. His face got redder. "A judgmental cap doesn't sit well on somebody who holds black masses and makes voodoo dolls!"

Donnie bristled.

"I'm sorry." Milton sat down and spread his hands palms upward. "It really got to me. What the hell, you never really expect something like that to happen to people you know."

"Why not?" Donnie snapped. "People it happens to have to be friends of somebody."

"Well sure, but . . . You don't like to think of anybody you know inspiring that kind of hate, that's all."

"Since when does a psychotic mugger need inspiration?"

"Mugger? What mugger?" Milton looked bewildered. "All I heard on the radio was that she was stabbed."

"Her jewelry was ripped off. You should read *The New York Times*."

"My God." Milton covered his face with his hands. This was no longer something that had happened to somebody he knew, it was SOMETHING THAT COULD HAVE HAPPENED TO HIM.

Or was he putting on an act? Even if he hadn't attended the party, he had known about it. He could have been the one who pinched my skewer and used it on Nina. As for motive, being on the receiving end of screw and run might be galling to a man who wasn't used to it.

Galling enough to fuel an explosion a couple of years later?

I was reaching for it. This was Milton Frankovich, affluent, good-looking, in prime physical condition (zealous jogging)—a guy who could assuage any ego blow in five minutes at any ballet studio in town. Not to mention the soft heart that has frequently moved him to treat patients who couldn't pay or to take a discarded girlfriend to Capezio and let her buy out the store. I might just as well try the murderer's hat on Donnie. No doubt I could make it fit. The same for practically everybody else I knew. At this very moment the police were probably trying to make it fit me. The whole thing seemed like a perverted game of pin the tail on the donkey.

Nonetheless, somebody had killed Nina with my skewer, and common sense said it had to be somebody I knew. No getting away from that.

Donnie and Milton had grooved into a gruesome amiability and were swapping notes on muggings-I-have-heard-about. All of a sudden it was too much for me. I pleaded a headache and asked if they would mind leaving me to myself. They reacted with a display of solicitude that should have made me ashamed of the lie, but I was beyond shame. I got the punishment I deserved, though. The minute they were gone, I felt so bereft I would have given anything to have them back. I puttered about with my usual Sunday morning clean-up. Next on the agenda should have been going for a long walk (good for the knee) and picking up *The*

New York Times on the way back. But if I went out I was bound to run into somebody all agog to talk about Nina. On the other hand, if I didn't go out, how would I get the paper?

The dilemma was resolved by Thea Davidson, ringing up to invite herself over. I said sure, if she would bring me *The New York Times*, and fifteen minutes later she arrived, looking her most Dragon Ladyish in black silk tunic and slacks. Along with the newspaper she brought homemade chicken soup, which went down far better than Donnie's herbal tea. Before I knew it I was spilling my guts. No matter that I knew every word I said would be all over town in a matter of hours, I simply couldn't shut up.

Thea heard me out in silence, the kohl-ringed eyes withholding comment, too. When I wound down, she didn't say anything right away. She inserted a cigarette into the long onyx holder, lit up, and inhaled as if she were drawing on the mouthpiece of an Aqua Lung. "I can see why you're worried. In your place I'd be quaking in my boots."

"Comforting." But I had to smile—anybody but Thea would have said "pissing in my pants."

"Looking at it objectively, though, there's no real evidence against you. Anybody could have taken the skewer at any time. The police are sure to find plenty of suspects and plenty of motives. Who do you know who's likely to clam up about Nina out of delicacy?"

"Now there's a lining of solid silver." But of course she was right. Most of the people we knew couldn't refrain from purveying gossip on pain of being strung up by their thumbs in the plaza of Lincoln Center.

"What strikes me as strange is that it should happen at this juncture," Thea said. "She'd mellowed out so. Hadn't offended anybody in ages, as far as I know. But perhaps you've heard differently?" Inflected, but it wasn't really a question. Any scuttlebutt would have reached Thea's ears long before mine—she was merely touching all the bases.

Donnie had raised the same point. Why would anybody want

to kill Nina now? For the past few months she had been immersed in courtship ritual, to a degree that barely allowed time for more than hello-good-bye to the world at large. Like a starry-eyed schoolgirl. Anybody would have thought she was embarking on her first marriage instead of her third.

"Of course, it might be something very, very new," Thea went on. "Perhaps Robbie found out about it and—"

"Hopped on a plane and sneaked into the building disguised as a six-and-a-half-foot rabbit? Be real, Thea."

"Naturally I'm not suggesting he did it himself. I was thinking more along the line of hiring it done. Apparently there's a lot of that sort of thing in his part of the country—you remember all those stories Nina used to tell."

"I think she made most of them up. But you're right. On paper, it's a theory. Still, Robbie putting out a contract on Nina? *Robbie?*"

Thea had to laugh. Around Nina, Robbie Beauchamp, an oversized, slightly over-the-hill Viking in cowboy boots, exuded—almost palpably—the kind of adoration big men seem to reserve for petite women. It was fatuous, it could be a little sick-making, but nobody ever doubted for a moment that it was genuine. They had met when Nina was married to her second husband, a Texas cattle baron, and Robbie had fallen for her hard. Quaintly, the idea of trying to take her away from another man hadn't entered his big, shaggy head (too much of a gent? some Texas fraternity taboo?); he removed himself from his oil fields and disappeared into the Alaska pipeline for several years. When he surfaced again, Nina's marriage was over, and he lost no time heading for Manhattan to begin his courtship. At first she regarded him as a joke, but he hung in there with dogged tenacity, and little by little his devotion earned him first tolerance, then a degree of reciprocation. A mismatch, everyone who knew Nina agreed, and most gave it from two to five years, tops.

"All right," Thea said. "I'll concede it's highly unlikely. But remember, Robbie has a family. Two grown daughters and a teenage son. Perhaps they didn't fancy Nina as a stepmother. And when it comes to families, we can't overlook Nina's own, can we? There's Anita, everybody's favorite den-mother-cum-doormat. And let's not forget little Shelley. You remember how upset she was when—"

"Give over, Thea. You're making me dizzy."

"Just trying to cheer you up, pet. Bear in mind that it's too early in the game to eliminate any motive, even robbery. Lots and lots of possibilities out there." Thea smiled widely, exhibiting teeth that sparkled in anticipation of chewing up those possibilities.

I was seeing barracudas all over the place. Saying that I felt hot and wanted to wash my face, I fled into the bathroom and locked the door. Not that I needed a lock against Thea, but I've known some who would follow me right in to continue a conversation. Nina used to do it all the time.

I didn't want to think about Nina. Not now. Not yet.

I splashed water on my face and examined my reflection in the mirror above the sink. My eyes, a changeable hazel, looked very dark and slightly glazed, like frosted tree bark. My nose and cheekbones and jaw jutted sharply out of flesh the color of unbaked biscuit dough. Put a babushka over my head and I could have played Anastasia's grandmother without makeup.

I ground my knuckles over my cheeks and brought up a little color. Splashing cold water and toweling dry brought up a little more. I didn't feel quite ready for another dose of Thea, so I sat down on the toilet seat to regroup. My glance traveled idly around the bathroom, stopped at the shelf above the bathtub. The lid of the tall alabaster jar I keep bath salts in was on backwards. Actually, the lid doesn't have a back or a front, just a crack running from knob to rim that I like the look of and always place to the front. Probably in my agitation last night I closed the jar any which way.

No. Last night I hadn't touched the jar at all. I had forgotten all about bath salts until it was too late. Which meant somebody else had been at the jar.

Ice slid down along my spine. I told myself I was being ridiculous. During the party, people had been popping in and out of the bathroom constantly. Somebody might have opened the jar out of curiosity. Or maybe the kind of somebody who puts antimacassars on chairs and doilies on tabletops had been disturbed by the crack and turned the lid around.

I got up, went over to the shelf, turned the lid around without lifting it, started for the door. The chill at my spine got chillier. I about-faced and went back to the shelf and lifted the lid. The scent of lemon rose to my nostrils from the yellow crystals heaped almost to the top of the jar.

An alarm bell went off in my head. *The last time I had used bath salts the jar had been only half full.*

I reached into the jar and my fingers closed over something hard and solid that definitely had not come from Caswell Massey. I drew it out. A watch. A slim platinum oval with a black face and diamond chips for numbers on a band of platinum links. A watch I had seen countless times on Nina Langlander's wrist. It was still ticking.

The sound was bothersome, and I held the watch at arm's length. But the sound seemed to get louder. I realized it wasn't the watch I was hearing, it was my heart. I squatted on the floor and emptied the jar onto the terra cotta tiles. Spilling out with the yellow bath crystals were a ring with a large, lustrous pear-shaped baroque pearl in a platinum setting and an antique amethyst-and-silver-filigree pendant on a slim silver chain. The ring I knew as well as I knew the watch. The pendant I had never seen before, but I could visualize it clearly at the V neck of the smoke-colored silk dress Nina had been wearing when she died.

I'd been right all along. There hadn't been any robbery. Whoever had killed Nina had taken the jewelry to make it look like one, then blithely sashayed into the john to hide it. Or maybe not so blithely. Maybe it had been a deliberate attempt to implicate me. No way of knowing. Either way, I was in heavy shit up to my ears.

One thing was for sure: I had to get the jewelry out of my house. Fast. Before the campfire Godfather and his minions paid me another visit, most likely armed with a search warrant.

It crossed my mind that if Tagliaferro had asked my permission to search the building yesterday I would have granted it. Why not? An innocent person has nothing to hide, right?

Ice slid down along my spine again.

A tap on the door. "Maggie, you've been in there almost twenty minutes," Thea whispered. "Is anything the matter?"

Panic made my head spin. I started to get up to lock the door, sank down as I remembered I had already locked it.

"Maggie?"

"I'm all right, Thea. Well, not entirely. As a matter of fact, I feel a sore throat coming on."

"Oh. *Oh.*" Thea, bless her heart, has a deep, abiding terror of germs. "Well, look, I'm running a bit late. Do you want me to fix you some lemon tea with honey before I go?"

"No, thanks. I'll heat up the rest of that chicken soup and tuck myself in—that should nip it in the bud. You don't mind letting yourself out, do you?"

"Of course not. Be sure not to let yourself dehydrate, Maggie. And keep warm. I'll ring you later."

I heard the clackety-clack of Thea's heels on the stairs. It seemed to go on for ages. When the front door closed, I got up and filled the sink with detergent and left Nina's jewelry to soak. Then I put on rubber gloves, swept up the bath crystals, and gave the bathroom floor a thorough mopping.

Still wearing the rubber gloves, I took the watch out of the sink and scrubbed it with a toothbrush. I scrubbed the ring. I scrubbed the pendant. I emptied the detergent out of the sink, put the jewelry back in, and ran the cold water for ten minutes. Nobody was going to get even a whiff of lemon from any of the pieces if I could help it.

The watch stood up to it all. Takes a licking and keeps on ticking. Naturally. What other kind would Nina have?

I took the watch and the ring and the pendant into the kitchen, dried them with paper towels, and put them into a doggie bag.

Now all I had to do was make them disappear.

Chapter 4

Maggie." Anita Langlander's blue eyes, a darker, more velvety blue than her sister's, opened very wide at the sight of me. "How kind of you to come."

I kissed her cheek and walked past her into the familiar foyer that always makes me think of an antechamber to a throne room. The floor is gray-veined black marble studded with silver stars, so it's the Queen of the Night you expect an audience with. And right away you come face to face with yourself in a full-length mirror with a heavy chased silver frame, the better to make you wonder if you're worthy of the audience. No place to sit down, needless to say. If you get tired waiting, well, what are knees for?

"May I take your things?"

"No, thanks. I'm not staying." I clutched my leather mailman's pouch a little closer to my side. "The last thing I want to do is add to your social burdens. You must have your hands full already."

"You could never be a burden, Maggie." Anita's smile was wan but friendly—not the kind you would bestow on somebody you suspected of wasting your sister. "Anyway, the crunch was yesterday. Traffic's light this morning, thank goodness. Only two boys who were in *Winter Dreams* with Nina and now you."

My heart sank. I had counted on a crowd to give me opportunity to plant Nina's jewelry somewhere in the apartment. The easiest method of disposal, of course, would have been a trash can, but I was afraid if the jewelry didn't surface the police might concentrate on robbery as a motive. I didn't want that. I wanted whoever killed Nina to pay.

"Not that I'm complaining, mind you," Anita went on. "People couldn't have been kinder. It's wonderful how they've rallied round, even the ones you wouldn't expect. I've been run off my feet."

The note of complacency in her voice made me take a good hard look at her. She was the very picture of grieving next of kin, dressed in a black wool sheath with a high round neck and long fitted sleeves, red-gold hair (a more subtly beautiful shade than Nina's, but who ever noticed?) in the impeccable braided coronet. Her face was pale and a little puffy and there were pink rims around her eyes, as if she had cried some and rubbed some but not a whole lot. I had the impression that she was shocked and distraught, yet not in the very depths of desolation.

"Oh, Maggie." Anita came up close and embraced me. The scent of lavender was strong in my nostrils. "I simply wasn't thinking. You probably need as much comforting as anybody, finding her like that. It must have been dreadful for you."

She steered me through the foyer and into the spacious, light-flooded French rococo living room, all pastels and fruit woods, gilt and ormolu and shellwork. My eyes sought out the mauve brocade armchair that had been Nina's favorite. Anita led me past it to a peach velvet settee. Seated, our backs were turned to the armchair.

"When I went to identify the—Nina, she looked so peaceful. You would never have guessed she'd been—" Anita bit her lip. "Was there a lot of blood?"

"No. The wound was very small. The bleeding must have been internal. I don't think she—" I broke off as a wave of nausea swept over me. I suddenly remembered that somewhere, some time, I had read that cows and pigs were butchered with skewers so their meat would be red.

Anita's face was bright with expectation. I had to look away from her. But my eyes took no comfort from the polished parquet floor, the richly muted oriental rugs. Least of all from the eve-of-guillotine furnishings.

"I don't think she suffered much." I forced myself to look at Anita again.

"They told me she didn't. They told me she was stabbed through the heart and must have died in a matter of seconds. That's a mercy."

"Yes." Idiotically, I found myself thinking about how many times I had heard people say Nina didn't have a heart. The nausea returned.

Beside me, Anita wriggled deeper into the settee and drew her legs up beside her, feet carefully extended over the edge so as not to soil the upholstery. "I've been driving myself round the bend, thinking that it might never have happened if I'd been a little more patient. She was on the phone with Robbie when Shelley and I were ready to leave for the party, and she said she'd be along later. I know she liked making an entrance, but with people she knew so well it wasn't that important. If we'd waited for her . . . But I was in a hurry because I was looking forward to the *zakouski*. Can you believe it?"

"Don't, Anita. What's the good?"

"I know it's pointless, but I can't let go of it. And I've been putting myself on the rack trying to remember whether anybody at the party behaved suspiciously—the police asked me that. But it's just as pointless, isn't it? I mean, everything points to a mugger, doesn't it?"

"Umm." The weight of my pouch seemed to increase a hundredfold.

"It must have been a mugger." Anita kicked off her shoes and tucked her feet under her. "Nina had her faults—I'd be the last person in the world to deny that—but she wasn't *wicked*. Nobody would ever have hated her *that* much."

She was overdoing it. By plenty. Sisterly loyalty or no sisterly loyalty, half a lifetime of supportiveness for someone who had never had to be told that it was a good thing to let it all hang out should have made her think twice about coming out with a statement as fatuous as that. Not to mention worry about her tongue falling out or her nose growing longer.

She read me pretty accurately. Her face took on a martyred expression. "All right. Nina was totally egocentric. All too often she behaved as if other people were around simply to be used or stepped on. As long as I'm at it, I might as well throw in that she didn't mind being a bitch for no reason at all. I know it. You know it. Everybody knows it. But can you see her doing anything so horrible that somebody killed her for it? I can't, and I probably knew her better than anybody else did. Except maybe you."

There was nothing to say to that. I couldn't really see it either. Yet somebody had killed Nina for a reason. I knew it hadn't been a mugging, even if Anita didn't.

Or pretended she didn't.

Not something I wanted to think about right now. I changed the subject. "How's Shelley holding up?"

"About the way you might expect. Why don't you look in on her, Maggie? I know she'd love to see you."

"I really don't have much time, Anita. I have tons to do before my afternoon classes and—"

"You can spare a minute or two, can't you? She'd be so

disappointed if you went away without saying hello." Anita was firmly back in the role of Little Mother.

I said okay and went out of the living room and into what was literally a marble hall, the floor the same gray-veined black marble of the foyer, the walls translucent white. Nina's whimsy. Her big party turn, which used to leave people in stitches, had been a throaty rendition of "I Dreamt That I Dwelt in Marble Halls," and when she bought the condo she decided "to make that idiotic dream come true so I'll never have to sing the damn song again."

I felt chilled now, as if I were traversing a glacier.

Shelley's door was closed. It took her a good minute to open up, and when she did she was visibly controlling her breathing. Starkly dressed in black turtleneck and tights and gray batik wraparound skirt, she looked lovely, with the ethereal radiance that seems unique to young dancers. The almost white coil of hair on top of her head shone like a halo above her slightly flushed face (if there's a drawback to being a real blond it's that your complexion rings all the changes), and I realized she'd been practicing. I was shocked—your basic Mrs. Grundy kind of shocked—and irritated with myself. Why shouldn't she be practicing?

"Hullo, Maggie. Nice of you to stop by." She sounded almost as if she meant it. One thing you can say for the child, she's mannerly. "Won't you come in?"

"Thank you." The instant my foot was over the threshold and I got a whiff of sweat overlaid with Arpège, I was sorry I'd let Anita bulldoze me. Ordinarily Shelley's room, situated at a corner, with enormous windows, is full of light, but today the indigo silk curtains were closed, and the illumination filtering through them would have suited a cabaret. Over the barre affixed to the wall hung a towel, soggy and limp, as if it had been soaking up a lot of sweat.

Shelley caught me looking at the towel and went rigid. "All

right. I was practicing." Defensive. Challenging me to reproach her.

Who was I to reproach anyone? I reached for the nearest platitude. "We all have our own ways of dealing with grief." It carried double the weight of banality because I saw no signs of grief about Shelley. The perfect oval face was totally self-contained and devoid of emotion (the way Myrthe, Queen of the Wilis in *Giselle*, is supposed to look when she's not being implacable), and it was hard to believe those clear blue eyes had shed many tears for her mother. Well, Nina hadn't been your typical doting mother; some said that battling Phil Russell for custody of Shelley was the one and only time she ever showed any maternal instincts. I recalled Shelley coming to me in tears, long after she had gone from my studio to the School of American Ballet, and telling me that her mother was getting married again and moving to Texas (the cattle baron) and insisted on taking her along. She didn't want to go, she would lose ground, she wanted to stay with her Aunt Anita in the condo and continue at SAB. Couldn't I do something? It was none of mine to intercede, but distress is distress, and I telephoned Nina. She could have told me to mind my own business, but she didn't. "Come off it, Maggie, I'm doing the kid a favor. We both know she's a good technician with a beautiful body. At NYCB she wouldn't go higher than the corps, but in a smaller puddle she could make all kinds of a splash." I couldn't dispute that assessment of Shelley's abilities. The marriage had lasted four years, and Shelley had zoomed back to SAB like a homing pigeon. Promotion to NYCB had come, but not advancement. For which she blamed her mother and those lost four years.

If the absence of grief wasn't exactly surprising, it was nonetheless disquieting. A party to celebrate Phyllis Cottman's landing a solo when Shelley had been passed over time and time again could well have fueled a lot of banked resentment. Suppose—

Those candid blue eyes were looking at me in bewilderment,

and suspicion died in me. Not that I couldn't imagine Shelley killing her mother. I could. It was the calculation I balked at. Pilfering the skewer. Removing the jewelry and planting it in my bathroom. It just didn't compute.

I looked at the towel again, then at the wall above the barre, where lithographs of Taglioni and Elssler and Vestris, posed studio shots of Pavlova and Nijinsky, state-of-the-art action shots of Suzanne Farrell in *Tzigane* and Baryshnikov in *Push Comes to Shove* vied with each other like dancers in a crowded studio. Every other time I had visited this room, there had been tights and leotards strewn about, point shoes lined up beside the open sewing basket, a full-length mirror on coasters facing the barre. The mirror was tucked away in a closet, the sewing basket closed, the point shoes and tights and leotards nowhere in sight. It was all as neat as the proverbial pin, except for the soggy towel.

My eyelids started to prickle, and for a moment I was afraid I might break down and cry. Here, in this hermetically sealed cocoon, I was thrust forcibly back into the past. My past. Nina's past. Every dancer's past.

I murmured condolences and practically fled the room. Nor did I dally taking leave of Anita; I was out in the hall striding to the elevator before she finished telling me how glad she was I'd come. About all I gleaned from the visit was a solid conviction that if either one of them had killed Nina, she was the reincarnation of Eleonora Duse. But I hadn't come to eliminate suspects, I'd come to get rid of the jewelry, and I'd failed.

Which meant going to Plan B. I walked over to Fifth Avenue and took the bus to midtown. I went first to the post office to buy twenty first-class stamps, next to a stationers to buy padded envelopes of diverse sizes, keeping my condolence-call gloves on for both transactions, then to the main branch of the New York Public Library, where I made straight for the ladies' room. Shutting myself up in a cubicle, I addressed one of the envelopes to Anita in block capitals with a magic marker, slipped the doggie-bagged jewelry inside, and sealed it with Scotch tape. I used the water in the toilet bowl to fix on the stamps (I know about saliva tests—no flies on me). I left the library and dropped the envelope into the nearest mailbox. My last port of call was Caswell Massey, to buy new bath salts. Jasmine, not lemon verbena.

Chapter 5

Down-two-three-four." I tapped the floor with my stick, punctuating Ravel's *Pavane for a Dead Princess* as my class did pliés. "Up-two-three-four. Your head and torso want to go upward, no matter how far down your legs go. Think of Persephone, pulled between two worlds. That's better. Very good, Judy. *Don't roll over the toe, Bridget!*"

A guilty rush of color submerged Bridget Foster's freckles, and several of the blameless flinched at my tone. Knee over the toe is one of the fundamental tenets of ballet, and cheating to make your turnout look wider is a cardinal no-no, unless you're keen on inviting trouble with your instep or your arches, muscle and tendon strain, and countless other woes. (A French horn player who attended my fundamentals class one day asked me if rolling over the toe could damage her embouchure and I told her very likely it could; she never came back.) If I added up the number of times I've berated students on this point alone, I'd get higher into mathematics than I care to go.

It wasn't the first time I'd lit into Bridget, a scrawny little fourteen-year-old with a straw colored pony tail and watchful, intelligent green eyes. The intelligence has rarely been displayed in my studio, where her concentration is so poor it's obvious she can't cherish any balletic aspirations. Why she comes to class I've always preferred not to think about. I gave her the glare that means "I'm-watching-you-like-a-hawk." Her face remained red, and I heard a few titters.

After pliés came battements tendus, and I didn't have to tell anybody not to sickle the foot—I saw nothing but taut arches and crisp points. The ronds de jambe par terre I called for next were equally impeccable. Watching my charges do their stuff, I found it hard to believe that only a little while ago, drained by my expedition to dispose of Nina's jewelry, I'd seriously considered canceling class rather than face them. Though the theater professionals in my morning classes had taken getting down to business in a place where a murder had occurred pretty much in stride, I had expected this gaggle of adolescents to act a bit jittery. No such thing. Performing développé now, they looked utterly pliant and relaxed, like sea anemones wafted by the current. I felt the stirrings of pride.

Talk about bad timing.

Away from the barre, things went from good to better. The adagio I gave was challenging, full of changing épaulement. Nobody got confused. Nobody's arms flapped like turkey wings. The kids all looked beautiful, so beautiful it brought a lump to my throat. This was more than an exceptionally good class. Something magical was happening, something I had experienced in the classroom only twice before, once as a student at Korovskaya's and once when I was teaching a class of dancers who could have leaped over the moon if I'd asked them to. How it could be happening during a class with Bridget Foster in it was totally beyond me, but happening it certainly was.

As I called out the steps for the closing allegro, I glanced at Mary Ann Sanders. Her eyes shone behind the rimless cheaters, her cheeks were tinged with pink, and wonder of wonders, a lock of pale hair had escaped from the pioneer woman knob. She plunged into the gigue of the fist Bach keyboard partita with gusto. Perfect choice. A truly splendid accompanist (light years ahead of any other I've had), she never requires advance discussion of the music. All I ever have to do is give a combination and the piano jumps in with the right bit of Beethoven or Mozart, Ravel or Poulenc, Chopin or Schumann, Bach or Purcell.

What goes up must come down. The drop was sudden. While my students were soaring, beating out entrechat quatre, something made me look over at the doorway, and I saw Sergeant Tagliaferro standing there.

The piano pounded to a stop. Movement came to a stop. Freeze frame. I wanted to freeze it forever. Instead, I blew a kiss to signal that class was over.

Nobody was in a hurry to leave. "That was the greatest class ever," said Judy Wilton, five feet six and all legs and still growing. The star of the class, which, unfortunately, isn't saying all that much.

"Thank you."

"Is he here to arrest you?"

"Shut up, stupid!" Bridget Foster grabbed Judy by the waist and dragged her toward the door. Judy smiled at me sheepishly and offered no resistance. Going out, she gawked at Tagliaferro. The rest of my students, playing it cooler, ignored him as they filed out, as if they took him for somebody who had come about the furnace or the cockroaches. He waited till they were all out of the room before approaching me.

"Your timing's excellent, Sergeant. This is the end of my teaching day."

He gave me a curt nod and glanced pointedly at the piano,

where Mary Ann lingered, still flushed and sparkly-eyed. She gave a start that you might call guilty, if you didn't know Mary Ann, closed the piano with a bang, and hurried out, her shoes loud on the floorboards. A moment later her footsteps clomped down the stairs.

Tagliaferro cleared his throat. "Bad news, I'm afraid. I'm here to search the building, Ms. Tremayne. I have a warrant." He reached inside his trenchcoat and took out a folded paper.

Inwardly, I thanked the gut instinct or lucky star or whatever it was that had sent me flying out of the house with Nina's jewelry at midday instead of waiting till my teaching day was over. Outwardly, I opened my eyes wide and acted surprise to the hilt. "What on earth for?"

"I can't divulge that." He was unfolding the paper.

I waved it aside. "You don't need a warrant. All you had to do was ask me. Try not to mess things up too much, will you?"

Something glinted in his eyes. In other circumstances, I would have taken it for amusement. "We'll try. As soon as the kids are out of the building, I'll bring my men in. I don't want to make this any harder on you than I have to."

He hardly sounded like a man hell bent on carting me off to the slammer, but there wasn't much comfort in that. Or in knowing that he wouldn't find what he was looking for. While he and two other plainclothesmen went through my apartment, I sat at the big round walnut table darning a pair of tights and trying to look unconcerned, glad I wasn't the center of attention because I didn't have all that much confidence in my performance. My mind was in turmoil. The fact that the police were here making this search indicated that hiding Nina's jewelry in my bathroom had been a deliberate attempt to implicate me. The killer must have expected it to be found right away, which would have meant my being arrested, or at least held for questioning. Since I was still walking around loose, the police had to be given a little help. An anonymous letter? More likely a phone call, made with a voice transformer or a mouthful of cotton or a handkerchief or—

It all seemed unbelievably hokey. Like a bad television cop show. But somebody had sicked the police onto me.

Who hated me that much?

It wasn't the first time I'd asked myself that question. But as long as I could construe stashing Nina's jewelry in my bath salts, like making use of my skewer to kill her, as doing what came handiest, I wasn't obliged to come up with an answer. Now things were different.

Were they? Maybe I had it all wrong. Maybe alerting the police to the whereabouts of the jewelry wasn't all that personal, merely a maneuver to focus attention in the wrong direction while the trail grew cold. Everybody knows that most homicides are solved within hours after they happen or chances are they don't get solved at all.

But what if I had it right? What if somebody really did hate me enough to try to frame me for murder? A real possibility, not something I could dismiss as paranoid fantasy. If only I could. If only—

"That coffee smells good. Got any to spare?"

I snapped out of it. The tights I was supposed to be mending were balled up in my left hand; my right was wrapped around a mug of stone cold coffee. Tagliaferro was standing a few feet away. How long had he been watching me? It didn't bear thinking about.

"Help yourself." I dropped the tights into the sewing basket on the floor beside my chair.

"Thanks." He went over to the stove, took a mug down from the rack, filled it from the coffee maker, came over to the table, and sat down. He chose his position nicely, northeast to my north—close enough to watch me carefully but not close enough to crowd me.

"What were you looking for?" The question any innocent person would ask. *Pour la forme.* I didn't expect an answer.

He surprised me. "We got a tip that we'd find Ms. Langlander's jewelry hidden in your apartment."

The way my stomach bottomed out, it might have been a news flash instead of confirmation of what I already knew. Deep down inside I'd been hoping against hope I was wrong. How childish can you get?

"What rubbish. Who told you that?"

It struck the right note: all that work to develop a stage persona hadn't gone for nothing. His response was a weary shrug.

"Oh, I see. An anonymous tip."

"That's right. The usual phone call from a voice that sounded like nothing human. Short and sweet, so we couldn't trace it. Everybody's an expert nowadays."

"All it takes is access to a television set. Did you really expect to find Nina's jewelry here? I mean, if I'd killed her and taken it as a smoke screen, do you think I would be stupid enough to hang on to it?"

"A tip is a tip. We have to check out everything." He swallowed coffee, set the mug down, gazed into it. "This is good," he said, and, with no change in tone, "Tell me about how Nina Langlander took your husband away from you." His eyes came up swiftly.

If he expected me to turn to jelly, I must have disappointed him. I picked up my mug and sipped from it, my hand steady as you please. "You really know how to go for the jugular, don't you? There really isn't much to tell. Yes, Nina did break up my marriage, and for years I hated her for it. But you can't keep on hating forever. We've been reconciled for quite some time now."

"For show or for real?"

"For real. But I don't suppose there's any way I can make you believe that."

"The grapevine backs you up. The word on it is that the past couple of years the two of you have been thick as thieves again."

"I don't know that I'd put it quite like that."

"How would you put it then?"

"The ballet world is small, Sergeant. Small and close-knit and pretty closed. If you belong to it, the other people who belong to it tend to count for more in your life than civilians, no matter how much you care for them. I loved my husband and losing him devastated me, but when he was gone he was gone. Nina was still around. And once upon a time we were very tight, primarily because we understood one another so well. After I cooled off it wasn't hard to slide into a groove again."

"Fair enough." He got up, picked up the two mugs, went to replenish them from the coffee maker, sat down again. His movements made me think of a dancing bear. "Tell me about Larry Sondergaard."

I should have seen that one coming. What more predictable than that he should ask about Nina's fling with organized crime? On paper, it looked like a hot lead. Only it wasn't.

"That's ancient history. I'm probably not the one you should be talking to about it—Nina and I were hardly sharing confidences when she got involved with him and—"

"I want to hear whatever you know or think you know."

"Nothing firsthand, I warn you. I never met the man, and she never talked about him." Mentally, I amended that. Nina had mentioned Larry Sondergaard to me once, remarking that he was surprisingly boring in bed for a man who was so dynamic everywhere else. I didn't feel obliged to pass that on.

"Skip the modest disclaimers, will you?" Tagliaferro had trouble keeping the irritation out of his voice.

"All right. She once had an affair with a gangster, if that's really the word for him. All I know about Larry Sondergaard is what everybody knows. Hearsay. The media. He rose from the streets and made himself into a gentleman of sorts. There's a veneer of gentility anyway. Collects art. Supports the New York City Ballet and the Metropolitan Opera and whatnot. Makes his dirty money from gambling, not prostitution or drugs, so I guess that makes him better than—"

"No such thing as 'better.' Gambling's his main source of income, but he dabbles in everything. He has to."

"I wouldn't know about that." Would Nina have known? Would she have cared?

"No, I guess you wouldn't. What are you trying to tell me, Ms. Tremayne? That they were Gatsby and Daisy?"

I had to smile "That's pretty good, Sergeant. Close to the mark, but not bang on. I think he might see himself as Gatsby. But Nina is—Nina was a long way from Daisy. I think she would have seen him seeing himself as Gatsby and been amused by it. Probably not the principal reason she got involved with him— I'm sure you've heard ad nauseam how acquisitive she was. Still, there was never a shortage of men eager to lavish their money on her, and she chose him. It didn't last long, but they parted on very good terms. I can vouch for that, in a way. I was having dinner at her place about a year ago when he telephoned to ask her advice about courting some socialite he was interested in. She reeled off a campaign plan that would have done credit to a general, and I could hear him laughing his head off at the other end. He must have paid attention, though, because he married his Daisy a few months ago. As you probably know."

"Yeah. Olivia Marsden." Tagliaferro twirled his mug gently on the table and glowered at it. "The captain just about went ape when Sondergaard's name cropped up. You can imagine. After that big, splashy wedding, an old girlfriend threatening to open one can of worms or another—Too good to be true, I guess. What can you tell me about the two ex-husbands?"

"I knew Phil Russell rather better than I wanted to. Your basic aspiring director with a talent that wasn't as big as his ambition or his ego, unfortunately for him. He and Nina were on-again, off-again, with a lot of detours on both sides, from her college days till she married him. I'm sure you've heard about the court battle for custody of Shelley. He was a pretty sore loser at the time, but for ages now he's been living on the West Coast, directing sitcoms and banging starlets. I should think he'd be hard pressed to remember why he ever wanted a daughter around in the first place. The cattle baron I never met. According to

Nina, he could be a real shit when he put his mind to it. After the marriage went sour and she was packing up, there was a burglary at the house, and she thought he staged it to repossess the jewelry he'd given her. If he did, he struck out, because she'd moved every last piece to a bank vault. The court proceedings were fairly amicable. She didn't ask for much of a settlement. Why should she have? The jewelry was worth a fortune."

Tagliaferro nodded, "That jibes with the reports we've had. The bit about the burglary is news, but if he didn't like being outsmarted over the jewelry the time to stick it to her was then, not now. Anyhow, he's just come through a divorce that was a whole lot nastier, which makes him an unlikely bet. Not that we can rule him out. Or anybody else." His dark, hooded eyes locked with mine, and I felt he could see everything that was going on in my head, ferret out all my secrets. I was suddenly sure he knew I'd found Nina's watch and ring and pendant and was about to tax me with it.

He broke eye contact and began twirling his mug again. "Did I happen to mention that my ex-wife is a ballet freak?"

I was so relieved my breath came out in a hiss. I tried to cover it with a laugh. "They're usually called balletomanes."

"Whatever. She remembers seeing you dance in the *Pas de Quatre*. The way she tells it, you were pretty hot stuff. She says you and Ms. Langlander used to do a takeoff on some old-time sister act that always brought down the house. Or is she confusing you with somebody else?"

Old-time sister act indeed. Ordinarily I would have let fly at such a description of the great Fanny Elssler and her sister, but not today. "Real balletomanes never confuse any dancer with somebody else."

"I guess not. Even I know clowning takes as much talent as playing it straight. Probably more. How did you happen to get into something like that?"

"Happenstance, you might say. There was a benefit for some Russian ballet teachers who had fallen on hard times, and Nina rounded up three other dancers and got Donnie Buell to choreograph a new version of the famous London *Pas de Quatre* that Perrot devised for Taglioni and Grisi and Grahn and Cerrito. The idea wasn't original—Keith Lester and Anton Dolin had done versions for Alicia Markova—but the parody was. We had a blast and so did the audience. Afterwards a theatrical agent came backstage and said if we put a full program together he could guarantee us bookings. Since none of us was exactly setting the ballet world on fire at the time, we didn't need much selling to go for it. We had a pretty good thing going until—I fell one night and tore up my knee. I'm sure the grapevine must have filled you in on that." I was mortified to hear the bitterness in my voice.

"Yeah. Tough break. I heard the others kept going for a while as a trio, but it never quite took. I guess you were their anchor."

"That's giving me too much credit. I did trouser roles and none of the others could replace me. Allie Joyce had the height and she tried hard, but as a cavalier she was a dud because she just plain outshone her partner. They probably could have found a replacement, but then our musical arranger died and Donnie went into a tailspin and—Well, you must have heard all about that."

"Yeah. What happened to the other two members of the *Pas de Quatre*, by the way? Nobody seems altogether clear on that."

"Out of sight, out of mind. Karin Holmquist went back to Minnesota to marry her childhood sweetheart. Allie Joyce—Allie stopped dancing. We haven't kept in close touch. Not much more than the annual exchange of Christmas cards, actually. I'm not big on reliving old memories." Understatement of the year. Of the decade. Of the century, perhaps.

"I can understand that." Tagliaferro got to his feet, and once again I thought of a dancing bear. "For whatever it's worth, my ex asked me to be sure to tell you she thinks it's ridiculous to suspect you of killing anybody."

"Are you always so scrupulous about honoring requests from

your ex-wife, Sergeant? Or is that just a little reminder that I'm still at the top of the list of suspects?"

"Rarely. And I don't have to remind you, do I? Thanks for your time, Ms. Tremayne. You'd better come down and lock up after me."

For all the lack of urgency in his tone, it was an order. Not one I felt like disputing, even if it did seem like protecting an empty barn. As I was bolting the door, it dawned on me that he had twice pronounced *Pas de Quatre* flawlessly, as if he had been rolling it around his tongue for years. His ex-wife the balleto-mane?

Was there really a balletomane ex-wife? Maybe Tagliaferro had done his homework thoroughly and was coming at me from an oblique angle to lull me into an illusory sense of security. The man was clearly capable of jerking people around like yo-yos when it suited him.

I found I believed in the ex-wife. Just as I believed he didn't take me seriously as a suspect. Why I believed I didn't know. Blind faith, very likely. Well, sometimes a little of that doesn't hurt.

What if I hadn't happened to find Nina's jewelry before he did?

That one sent a chill traveling from my coccyx up to the nape of my neck. Never mind. I'd found the jewelry and I'd got rid of it—that was the bottom line.

I went up the stairs and into the studio. In the waning daylight the big, lofty room looked peaceful, as if it were resting up. Death had come and gone without a trace. No tell-tale stain had seeped into the floorboards. No bad vibes had disturbed my classes. Art is long all right. And totally selfish.

I looked at the mirror, all silvery in anticipation of moonlight; at the piano shut up tight; at the visitors' bench. I had what I'd come for. I turned to leave. In my sight line was the hall window, tall and narrow and divided in four by what looks like an upside down crucifix. The light behind the glass was pink, more like Homer's rosy-fingered dawn than like approaching twilight. A fluke, but for a moment it turned my time sense topsy-turvy, and I had the sense that life was beginning all over again. My heart gave a flutter, though I knew full well that if the Lilac Fairy or some other enchantress could wave a magic wand and give me my life to live over again, it would take exactly the same direction.

What makes a dancer? What makes somebody say, "My body is my canvas, my pen, my lyre, and with it I'm going to create the world?" In other ages—the ages of the immortals, if you like—dancers didn't think in those terms. They didn't choose their careers out of a sense of mission (the only one who claims to is Pavlova); they apprenticed to a trade members of their families had often followed before them, and they expected to make a living at it and mostly did. In present-day America, dancing is a vocation. You go into it knowing it means an investment of time and money you probably won't get full return on, knowing there's no certainty of job prospects, let alone job security. Throw in that dancers have to concentrate on developing their bodies when others are developing their minds, that the time in the sun is brief, that all too often a tundra of faded hopes lies on the other side.

So why? I can pose the question, but damned if I can answer it. I was that living cliché, the girl who decides from go that she wants nothing better in the whole wide world than to dance. "Go" came from my mother, who was bitten by the ballet bug while seeing Pavlova and Diaghilev's Ballets Russes and became an ardent champion of Lucia Chase, Lincoln Kirstein, and George Balanchine, though the last tried her patience by "mucking about" on Broadway and in Hollywood. Naturally her children had to have ballet lessons. My brother Eric balked, but the moment I walked into the Thompson Street loft redolent of anise (there was a bakery underneath) where Miss Francine Marza put her classes through their paces, I felt I belonged. Which doesn't mean I have happy memories of the place. Far from it. I recall once getting careless during plié and letting my shoulders slouch ("The upper part of your body must be immune to the law of gravity. Think that there's a wire between your shoulder blades pulling you up to the sky even when you're trying to touch your bottom to the floor"). Miss Francine didn't bother with a verbal correction, she rammed her stick inside my leotard and I had to finish the barre with an extra spine, feeling like Helen Burns in *Jane Eyre*, who had to wear a band labeled "Slattern" around her forehead. This was by no means the only time I had cause to confuse that loft with Lowood—Mr. Brocklehurst would have approved of Miss Francine's regime. Above the spinet, presided over by Miss Theresa Marza (sister? cousin? I never knew) was a cross-stitch sampler: NEVER EXPECT THANKS FROM YOUR PUPILS. Miss Francine, dark and elegantly long of limb, had done a stint in a pioneer ballet company in Chicago and worked on Broadway in the days when friends of producers outnumbered dancers in chorus lines. It didn't add up to much of a career, and being reduced to teaching too early had made her bitter, but she was meticulous about the right things and you left her hands with the most solid of foundations.

And leave her hands you did, because she literally threw you out. When I was fourteen, she kept me after class one day, handed me a piece of paper, and said, "This is where you take class from now on." On the paper was an address in the West Fifties. No name. No telephone number. "There's no such thing as staying in the same place," Miss Francine went on. "You go forward or you go backward." I took the paper and the message home, where they touched off quite a brouhaha. My father, who had a deep and abiding love for music, might have accepted dedication to the cello, but he regarded ballet (like opera) as a hybrid, therefore intrinsically worthless. My mother, although a balletomane, was in no sense a ballet mother; a second-generation graduate of Radcliffe, she saw higher education as woman's destiny. Realizing that Miss Francine's push was toward total commitment, both my parents, abetted by my brother and all the relatives they could enlist, went to work laughing my balletic aspirations to scorn. Everybody knew dancers are lovely to look at but when they open their mouths bubbles come out; everybody knew dancers' lives are short on performances and long on memories; everybody knew there was no demand for six-foot ballerinas. The bombardment was steady and unrelenting.

I don't suppose the outcome was ever in doubt, though. From the time I was old enough to sit still in a theater, I had been going to ballet performances, and back then American ballet was young, pulsating with life, and habit-forming—just ask anybody who grew up on it. In the splendor of the old Metropolitan Opera House, I watched *Giselle* with vintage Markova and with Alonso, too (it was the era when some wag remarked that if you wanted to dance the role and your name wasn't Alicia, you were a non-starter), and Nora Kaye in *Pillar of Fire*. At the New York City Center, where you could hear the dancers' shoes thud and squeak on the stage floor, I watched Maria Tallchief flash and dart in *Firebird* and got a frisson every time Tanaquil LeClercq drew those black gloves over her long, pale arms in *La Valse*. I wasn't conceited enough to imagine myself rivaling any of those goddesses, but I could imagine myself up there on the stage with them, if I worked hard enough.

All I needed, to commit myself body and soul, was a little nudge from fate. I got it, or thought I did, which amounts to the same thing. One rainy morning, instead of walking to the IRT subway station for the train that would take me directly to my school on the Upper West Side, I opted for the closer BMT station and changing trains at Times Square. There, waiting for my train, was a slim but powerful looking man with coppery skin and dark hair and eyes and assertive, memorable cheekbones. I recognized those cheekbones. Hadn't I seen *The Moor's Pavane* four times? He was José Limón. Nobody was paying him any attention, and I wondered how he could take being ignored so calmly. He was a dancer; he was *important*. On the train I stood as close to him as I dared, my heart going sixteen to the dozen, in a state of such exaltation I was tempted to stay on past my stop. But this was life, not "The Trolley Song." I got out at my usual stop and went on to school. The very next day I presented myself at the address Miss Francine had given me. It was the studio of Maria Ivanova Korovskaya, tall and heavy and sibylline in a deep purple caftan and a black turban. Piercing black eyes measured every inch of me, and she muttered something in Russian and waved me to the dressing room.

I became aware that the light beyond the hall window had altered, darkened. No more illusion of dawn. Night-blooming pink now. The same light I saw the first time I looked at that window, when I felt as if I'd stepped into Georgia O'Keeffe's *Fifty-ninth Street Studio*. Around me then had been a bleak expanse of empty space, used for storage by the previous owner of the building, an antiques dealer. A beleaguered and battered sense of possibilities stirred inside me. I decided this was the building I had to have, even though I'd looked at several others in far better condition. I designed the studio myself. Handpicked the pine boards for the floor and the rosewood for the barres; watched over every step of the construction so that the workmen became sick of the sight of me. Setting up shop gave me a center again, yanked me out of the what-the-hell-do-I-care cycle of dissipation and promiscuity I had drifted into.

Slowly the pink light deepened to purple, and I found myself looking out at a night sky. I walked out of the studio and up the stairs, feeling somehow that I was going to ground.

Chapter 6

Nina's funeral service was held on Saturday in an Upper East Side chapel with mahogany paneling and stained glass windows and an ambiance muted and ceremonious and calculated to keep manifestations of grief under control. The whitewood and pewter coffin resting in a bower of orchids and lilacs and violets was closed. The *Introit and Kyrie* of the Fauré *Requiem* was being piped in softly when I arrived, a bit tardy because I was trying to dodge making conversation. The chapel was practically full, and I slipped into a seat near the back, among people I didn't know.

The minister, tall and stringy and gray of hair and skin, was a murmurer. He murmured of sorrow that was not sorrow, of being called by God to glory everlasting. He didn't make the life hereafter sound very enticing, and none of what he said seemed to have much relevance to Nina. When he wound down, Suzanne Danco's voice floated out over the room in the *Pie Jesu*. The right requiem, the right performance—trust Anita for that.

People started moving out of the chapel in orderly fashion. Up ahead I spotted Donnie Buell's cap of silver hair and thought about pushing forward and catching up with him, but decided against it. Outside, a pallid March sun was fighting through a gray sky. Earlier it had been raining lightly, and there were damp patches on the sidewalk, but the fleet of limousines waiting to transport people to the cemetery didn't have a speck of moisture on them. I saw Thea Davidson not far ahead of me, and again could have caught up easily and didn't. I got into a limousine with a group of people I didn't know who didn't know me. While muted voices talked of futures and the unfavorable trade balance with Japan, I thought about the last time I'd seen Nina, the day before Angela's party, hurrying across the plaza of Lincoln Center to hail a cab. She hadn't seen me, and I hadn't called out to her because of course I was going to see her at the party the next evening.

Now I would never see her again.

Who would ever have thought it would matter so much? The first time I set eyes on Nina Langlander, she walked into my Freshman English class at Barnard, and I wished with all my heart she would walk right out again. The lapis lazuli eyes, the coil of Moira Shearer red hair, the petite small-boned build that was perfect for a sylphide's wings—just looking at her made me feel like an overgrown klutz. I managed to avoid her until the day we had to hand in, on three by five cards, our choice of a minor nineteenth-century literary figure as the subject of a paper. The instructor, a callow specimen addicted to tweeds and much fiddling with an unlighted pipe, riffled through the cards, smiled condescendingly, and said, "Well, well, well. In a class of twenty-three, two people want to write about Théophile Gautier. I call that finding a minor figure with a magnifying glass." My eyes met Nina's, and the indignation I saw there reflected what

I felt. Gautier, after all, had written the scenario for *Giselle*, championed Taglioni and Elssler and Grisi—his criticism had made ballet respectable. Nina came up to me after class and said, "The supercilious bastard is going to get the two best damn papers he ever saw." Maybe they weren't, but they were good enough to get us A's. I majored in English, Nina in Fine Arts with quite a few electives in English, and the two of us became rather celebrated in the English department, which probably found out more than it really wanted to know about such matters as David Garrick's championship of Noverre in the face of anti-French riots, the reactions of Emerson, Longfellow, and Margaret Fuller to Fanny Elssler's visit to America, the swathe Lydia Lopokova cut through Bloomsbury.

If Nina and I hadn't been dancers, would there have been anything to draw us together? Might as well ask whether people with type AO blood really have anything in common. In more ways than you could count we were chalk and cheese. Even in our dancing. Nina studied with Akhsanova, who stressed bravura and brio, in contrast to Korovskaya, for whom the sine qua non of movement was legato. Nina was gregarious; I was anything but. She could walk into a room full of people and pick off any man who struck her fancy; I was a late bloomer sexually, hardly aware of my body as anything but a dancer's instrument until I was past twenty. If you want to reach for it a bit, you could say we were both rebels. Much as I flouted a bluestocking ethic, Nina delivered herself from a gilded cage. Hers was robber baron stock a couple of generations on, after cash register had segued into social register: "A railroad merged with a bank and instituted Anita and me" was the way she put it. When she was barely out of diapers, her mother (the railroad) ran off with a Brazilian coffee planter, and the replacement was mad about ballet, hence the lessons that eventually led to the spurning of coming out parties, Junior League, and the rest of the debutante scene.

The drive to the cemetery was over before I knew it, and presently the coffin was being lowered into the ground. A feeling of desolation swept over me with the force of a physical blow. The minister started murmuring again, the bit about all flesh being grass, and I recalled Nina's telling me long ago that she didn't want to go to grass, she wanted to be cremated and have her ashes strewn over the Atlantic. Had she changed her mind? Doubtful. She'd never been one for changing her mind once she'd made it up. More likely somebody had overridden her wishes.

Who? I looked over at the family party assembled beside the grave. Nina's father and stepmother, spare and silver-haired and impeccably preserved. An overblown woman in a billowing black cloak with a flaming, purple-shadowed mass of hair and arms full of orchids, presumably Nina's mother. Anita and Shelley, arm in arm. Standing a little apart, Robbie Beauchamp, in well-worn black cowboy regalia (according to Nina, his wardrobe consists of a trunkful of old Gary Cooper costumes he bought at an auction), the breeze ruffling his salt and pepper hair as the tears poured down his cheeks. My money was on Daddy and Stepmama to have vetoed cremation. Not Anita, who had brought Fauré into the chapel and kept out lilies, which belong in Act Two of *Giselle* and nowhere else. Unthinkable that it could have been Robbie, and Mama looked the sort who would have insisted on scattering the ashes herself.

The minister stopped murmuring. With a prodigious groan, Mama flung her armload of orchids into the grave. She began to sob and was led away by a spare, silver-haired man who might have been Daddy's twin brother. A couple of men with shovels pushed through the crowd and began heaving earth into the grave as if they had a train to catch. Daddy and Stepmama and Anita and Shelley and Robbie all stood fast, but others, apparently confused by the change in tempo, started edging away. In a matter of moments the orderliness characterizing the proceedings up to then went by the board in a general rush for the limousines. Not a stampede exactly, but very unseemly, with a fair amount of pushing and shoving. A scene, it occurred to me, that Nina would have relished.

Desolation swept over me again. God, I was going to miss Nina. Never again would I be able to share a laugh with her. Which may sound like a small thing, but it isn't, it isn't, it *isn't*.

I turned away from the grave and found a long black arm barring my way. Then I was looking at the bronzed, seamed face of Robbie Beauchamp, at smoldering anthracite eyes that made me feel like the snake in the grass about to take the full brunt of the marshal's wrath.

"Listen up now, little lady," he boomed. "The cops are damn fools. If they had half a grain of horse sense they'd never think you could have had anything to do with killin' Nina. They give you any trouble, you let me know. Hear?"

Everybody heard. Everybody stopped moving to listen up.

"Thanks, Robbie."

"Don't mention it. Nina thought the world of you, Maggie. Look after yourself now." A big black-gloved hand patted my shoulder, and Robbie strode away, the crowd parting like the Red Sea.

I was subjected to a bombardment of inquisitional stares.

An arm slid round my waist. "Not to worry, little lady," Donnie Buell murmured in my ear.

"Don't *you* 'little lady' me!"

People moved away from us. Fast.

Donnie smiled mischievously at me. He had foregone his usual gray threads in favor of a black officer's greatcoat with crucifix-embossed pewter buttons, worn with the collar turned up against a nonexistent wind—perfect getup for the duel scene in *Eugene Onegin*. "Sorry, love. I couldn't resist."

"Obviously."

"In our virago mode, are we, love? So valiant of us." He lowered his voice. "We need to talk. Can you stop off at my place for a tête-á-tête?"

"Tête-á-tête? That's quite a vote of confidence."

"Don't overdo it, Maggie. This is important."

The prospect of lending an ear to Donnie's moans and groans

held little charm, but I couldn't refuse the naked appeal in his eyes. I said yes, and we rode back to Manhattan in the same limousine. Again the other passengers were strangers to me, except for a quondam swain of Nina's who sobbed and sniffled noisily all the way. Just the sort of behavior that would normally elicit a sarcastic comment or look from Donnie, but all he did was gaze out the window. I had ample opportunity to observe that his face looked fragile and worn, the wrinkles at the corners of his eyes and mouth like hairline scars; also frighteningly vulnerable.

Donnie's pad is a duplex comprising the top two stories of a brownstone off Columbus Avenue, the two stories made one over an area about thirty feet by forty and devised to look like an indoor courtyard. White walls and almost invisible white doors. White tile floor strewn with white hassocks and giant white pillows. At the top, a huge skylight, track lights, and speakers suspended by wires Astrodome-style. A pair of steel spiral staircases lead to an upper-story walkway, supported by steel girders and railed by more steel.

"I need fortification after all that fresh air," Donnie announced, and opened the door to the kitchen, a long, narrow room, very bright (four big windows), brimming with equipment, everything from wood-burning stove and metate to microwave and Cuisinart. "How does a bourbon flip sound?"

"Terrific," I lied, bracing myself for the worst. For Donnie, alcohol is the last of last resorts. While he betook himself to the giant butcher block counter, I went over to the dining counter, a chunk of knotty pine that looks as if it came out of a chow house for loggers, and perched on a high three-legged stool with my back to the preparations.

By and by the blender whirred, stopped, and then a crystal goblet filled with pale amber froth was set down in front of me. The fumes from the bourbon were almost strong enough to erode my nostril membranes.

"Not here." Donnie stalked out of the kitchen, the tails of the operatic greatcoat flapping. I picked up my goblet and followed him out of the kitchen and across the courtyard to the rear staircase. My heart sank as I realized we were heading for the shrine.

Not many people have shrines in their homes. Not many more would even conceive of having shrines in their homes. With Donnie, there's never much of a jump from conception to actualization. The shrine has nothing to do with religion. It's a room consecrated to Terry Sablier, dead these past two decades. Terry was the *Pas de Quatre*'s musical arranger, conductor when he could fit it in (he was much in demand), even pianist on a couple of orchestra-less occasions. To say he was the love of Donnie's life is perhaps to understate the case. In the closet are a midnight blue suit and a tuxedo, Terry's work clothes, and the denims and cords and chinos, the T-shirts and army surplus khaki shirts, the sneakers and desert boots and Chicago Cubs baseball cap he really lived in. A small bookcase and half a dozen music cabinets house his library. One wall is a montage of photographs.

I looked at the centerpiece of the montage, a twice life-size portrait of Terry, lank hair freshly trimmed, pale blue eyes making an effort to focus on the here and now, sweet shy smile for the camera. A portrait that makes you think nobody could ever be as nice as this. But he could be. He was. Everybody adored him. Not that he was perfect. He had his foibles, and some of them could irritate the hell out of you. Like his evangelical fervor when he preached the gospel of chemical-free diet and health care. Or worse, his meanness about money. He earned tons of it, but you would never have guessed it to look at him. And of course he never carried cash, so if you went out to dinner with him you found yourself paying the check and listening to promises to pay that were kept only if you pressed, and most of his friends didn't have the heart to press. The meanness, which didn't extend beyond money (if you happened to admire something he owned he would like as not give it to you on the spot, and he was lavishly generous with his time), was obviously rainy-day orientation gone mad; practically everything he earned went into the bank. Donnie, who thought the main purpose of money was to buy comfort and pleasure, used to complain about it all the time.

I slid my eyes away from that beamish smile and found something even more painful to look at. Myself. Smiling, too. Part of a happy quartet that patently had everything going for it, grouped around a table gazing rapturously at Terry, who appeared to bask in our adoration like a sultan in a harem of wayward Pollyannas (if you had trouble believing wayward of Karin Holmquist's angelic blondeness, you could believe anything of Allie Joyce's carved ebony profile). A very stagy photograph. How could it not have been? We were all acting up a storm as a favor to Terry, who wanted to end his marriage without coming out of the closet. There were hurts and hurts, he told us, and that was one he didn't want to inflict on his wife or on his family back somewhere in the heartland; much better to let them all think the big city had turned him into Don Giovanni reincarnate. A harmless deception we were perfectly willing to go along with.

Would things have turned out differently if we hadn't been so obliging? Not long after I tore up my knee, Terry swallowed a bottleful of barbiturates hard on the heels of a quarrel with Donnie. Ostensibly, the quarrel—one of many—was over Donnie's cruising, but I've often wondered whether the fundamental discord wasn't over Terry's refusal to come out and live openly with Donnie. The cynical maintain that most suicides are intended to punish the living, and if punishing Donnie was what Terry had in mind, he did a bang-up job. Overnight, the first wrinkles appeared on Donnie's face and the first welts on his body, and he seemed to take a giant step on the causeway linking Ganymede and painted queen.

"Odd you should zoom in on that picture," Donnie said. "Nina was in here just before Christmas, and she couldn't keep her eyes off it either."

I turned away from the past to look at him, squatting on a sleeping bag in the corner, cradling the bowl of his goblet with both hands. I went over to sit beside him. "Nina was here? In this room?"

He nodded. "Marched right in cool as you please. Eerie, isn't it?"

"Strange, anyway." Sentimental reverence for the departed had never been Nina's thing, and she thought Donnie's shrine obsessive and unhealthy. "Did she give you any reason?"

"She said she was in the mood to reminisce about the group. I didn't really believe that—Nina wasn't one for nostalgia—but I have to admit she put on a good show. Asked a ton of questions. Said she wanted to find out if I remembered things she'd forgotten."

But Nina had a memory like an elephant. "What kind of things?"

"Gossip, mostly. The kind of stuff people say behind your back. I suppose she thought being behind so many scenes I might have heard things she hadn't. Well, I dredged up every spiteful remark I could recall, but it didn't amount to diddly, and anyway I had the impression she was hearing it all for the umpteenth time. I said as much to her, and she said she wanted confirmation of details so she'd have some nice juicy tidbits about her past to give the Texas matrons an earful. I must say I found that totally unconvincing."

So did I. Nina had never been known to let a triviality like sticking to the truth spoil a good story. And anyway, it was going to be second time round with the Texas matrons.

"I mentioned it to the fuzzies—they wanted to hear about anything that seemed the least bit out of character—but they didn't think it was anything much. To be candid, neither did I until I found myself standing at the grave today and— Do you suppose she might have had a premonition?"

"Why ask me? Or do you think I ought to be having one, too? As far as I know, New York hasn't reestablished the death penalty. But maybe you know something I don't."

"For God's sake, Maggie!"

"Sorry. I'm edgy." I took a swallow from my goblet. The taste of cream and honey laced with vanilla and cinnamon and nutmeg made me think of a posset for the hypochondriac, but the quantity of bourbon took it out of Mr. Woodhouse's league.

Why had Nina visited this room and pumped Donnie about the past? She must have had a reason. Nina never did anything without a reason.

Was Donnie right? Had she been prompted by something that had nothing to do with reason? Call it whim, impulse, premonition, whatever? I couldn't really buy into that.

I looked at the montage again, at the photograph of the *Pas de Quatre* and Terry gathered round the table. Terry was dead. Nina was dead. Karin might as well have been on another planet. As for Allie, I never thought about where Allie was if I could possibly help it. Which left only me around and kicking.

"A penny for 'em, Maggie."

"No sale. Not even if you offered a Susan B. Anthony dollar. Or a petal from Nijinski's *Spectre of the Rose* costume."

"Well, I'm certainly not about to offer *that*." Donnie smiled. "I knew I could count on that tongue of yours as a counter-irritant to the blues. Thanks."

Sacking out in another room would have served the purpose better, but I kept the thought to myself. "For what? You know, this might be a good time to call Willie and have him line up some gigs for you." Donnie's choreographic skills have always been in demand for arranging fights, crowd scenes, and suchlike for the stage and the screen.

"Busy work?" Donnie's smile became a little broader. "Actually, darling, I've got almost more on my plate than I can handle. Did I ever tell you about the commission I accepted to stage something for a youth correctional facility in New Jersey? Probably not. I put it on a burner so far back I forgot all about it. This morning I got a wake-up call from the warden's PR director or whatever she is and would you believe the time is now? Or almost. I'm practically at my wits' end. But then I got into the shower to cogitate and this tiny idea came to me. Why not stage a version of *The Sleeping Beauty* in terms the little punks can understand? A real challenge, and I really think I've figured out how to meet it. That's the other reason I lured you here. You're the perfect sounding board."

I groaned mightily, because I knew that was what he expected. Actually, I didn't mind being a sounding board. Anything was preferable to the orgy of lamentation I had anticipated, even listening to a scenario for trashing the most magical ballet in the literature. A detailed scenario—that shower had certainly been a long one.

Chapter 7

I am sitting on a bus that is moving down Broadway. Slowly. At a snail's pace. Junior is beside me. Close beside me. My arm is tucked underneath his. Our legs touch all the way from thigh to ankle. My cheek is pressed against his, and each time he takes a breath my nostrils quiver. Around us, empty seats and plenty of space, so we can say anything we like to one another. We aren't saying anything.

Suddenly Junior pulls his head away from mine, and a pang of loss stabs my heart. But he's only drawing back to fix those dark amber eyes on me. He smiles. My eyes banquet on the high cheekbones Donatello would have loved, the cornsilk hair that sunlight turns to gold.

The bus stops. A woman gets on, hurtles to a seat, and plops herself down next to a man in a sheepskin coat. He has a gaunt, hawksbilled face. I know that face almost as well as I know my own. He is George Balanchine. He must have been on the bus for some time. Amazing I didn't spot him sooner.

The woman proceeds to harangue Mr. B. A ballet mother. In a flap because her darling daughter isn't advancing at SAB as rapidly as she should, or as rapidly as Mama thinks she should. Only the occasional word reaches my ears, but I have no trouble filling in the blanks. On behalf of all the dancers Mr. B has ever deemed unworthy of his favor—too tall or too short or too stocky—I exult. I hope Mama will keep him squirming on the hook for a while.

But he isn't squirming. He catches my eye and gives me a faint, quizzical smile. He doesn't know who I am, but he knows what I am, which amounts to the same thing. I smile back in spite of myself. We're fellow conspirators, in league against Mama.

Junior gives my arm a quick squeeze. "Time to get off."

He stands up and heads for the door. I start to get up to follow him, but my knee buckles and I sink down again.

"Junior. Wait for me."

He doesn't hear me. He's at the door now. The bus stops. The door opens. He steps down and gets off without a backward glance. The bus starts moving again, and all I can see of him is the top of his sun-gilded head. And then I can't even see that.

I look for Mr. B, but he's gone, too. So is Mama. So is everybody. The only passenger left on the bus is me.

"I want to get off," I say at the top of my voice. I stand up. My knee buckles again, but I shift my weight on to the good leg and do a sequence of poor man's glissades to the door and pull the wire for the buzzer.

The buzzer doesn't buzz. The bus doesn't stop.

"I want to get off. *Right now.*"

The bus keeps moving. I turn to glare at the driver, but there's nobody in the driver's seat. The bus is driving itself. Not fast, thank God. At a snail's pace, like before.

Maybe I can force the door open. I push as hard as I can. No go. The doors are programmed to remain shut when the bus is in motion. Outside, I see dancer after dancer, free as a bird in flight. How long am I going to be stuck here? Maybe forever. Maybe this is Sartre's *No Exit* revised by Andy Warhol.

Suddenly the bus bucks like a bronco and I'm flung against the door. Pain shoots through my knee. There's a ringing in my ears, loud and shrill . . .

The telephone woke me. I was shivering. My knee was throbbing. With remembered pain, not present pain. There's a world of difference.

I drew the pillow over my head to drown out the ringing. I was grateful to the caller for getting me off that bus, but not that grateful.

Odd about my nightmares. They generally begin with a real memory. Junior and I did have that chance sighting of Mr. B, but we got off the bus while he was still getting an earful from Mama. Apparently I can't let go of the detritus of real life even when I'm asleep. Something there for a shrink, no doubt.

I had exorcised Junior from my thoughts years ago. A real bummer if he were to start invading my dreams again.

The full title is Alexander Parkington, Jr., but he's been known as "Junior" since the age of six, when he stopped being Alexander Parkington III; before that he was Sasha, very briefly, his novel-reading mother not having been around long enough to make it stick. Alexander I, who parlayed a respectable fortune into an obscene one during World War II (munitions, I think— nobody ever discussed it and I didn't really want to know), was, from all accounts, your archetypical iron-willed patriarch, and he seems to have taken the iron with him. All his son and grandson inherited was the money, too much to piss away no matter how hard they try, and they certainly do try. Alexander II embarked on a wife-collecting career practically the minute the patriarch was underground; the last time I counted he had drawn even with

Henry VIII, but that was a while back. Like father, like son. Only Junior is leery of marriage.

He did, however, marry me. We were young. Neither one of us knew any better.

The phone kept on ringing. Stubborn, whoever it was. So am I. I kept on not answering. Sunday morning belongs to me, come what may. The second onslaught of ringing began while I was in the middle of my ablutions and didn't stop until I was almost finished taping my knee.

The siege shifted to the doorbell while I was eating breakfast. With a glass of grapefruit juice, two bites of toast, and half a cup of coffee inside me, I decided I was up for opening the door. My visitor was Mary Ann Sanders, decked out in a long charcoal gray fitted coat, black watch cap, and black boots, which was very likely her regular going-to-church outfit but made her look like a committed sixties hippy on her way to plant a bomb in Lord and Taylor or something. Was she the one who had been giving my telephone a workout since the crack of dawn? I was inclined to doubt it. More likely I had action on another front to look forward to.

"You're out and about bright and early, Mary Ann. Come in, won't you."

"Thank you." She stood aside to let me precede her up the stairs, as if I were a decrepit maiden aunt, and followed on soundless feet. Rubber soles on the boots, no doubt, but a little spooky nonetheless, like having a detached shadow behind me. On the turn of the studio landing, I cast a surreptitious glance over my shoulder to make sure she was really there.

The phone started ringing again the instant I came in the door, and I went straight to it. Thea Davidson, primed to rehash the funeral.

"Can't talk, Thea. I have company. I'll call you back in a few minutes. Okay?"

Hanging up, I realized how rude that "few minutes" sounded, as if I could hardly wait to get rid of my company. So naturally

76

I had to knock myself out trying to be hospitable; accompanists like Mary Ann don't grow on trees. She declined an offer of coffee. Tea? Herbal tea? Cocoa? All were declined with thanks. She did accept an invitation to sit down and went so far as to open the top button of her coat. Then she seemed to turn into a statue, simply sitting there and staring at me. I couldn't read anything in those pale blue eyes, flattened and depthless behind the rimless glasses, and yet I had an impression of calculation. But what was she totting up?

I had an overpowering sense of déjà vu. Last summer, a few weeks after Mary Ann started playing for me, I needed to reach her in a hurry and her phone was out of order, so I trekked up Riverside Drive to her apartment near Columbia University. Her building was one of those expansive brick relics of the twenties, subdivided into a rabbit warren. I had to ring her bell twice before a mistrustful "Who's there?" came over the intercom. She buzzed me into one of those prehistoric big lobbies, musty smelling and crowded with a job lot of overstuffed armchairs and tables that looked as though they had been forgotten in people's attics for thirty or forty years. Mary Ann's living room smelled of lavender, not mold and mange, and the furniture wasn't shabby, but the atmosphere was just as claustrophobic. The dimensions were about fifteen by eighteen, and in addition to the Steinway there were a garnet plush sofa suite and enough cabinets, tables, lamps, and whatnot to furnish a room twice the size. I felt I was being smothered by proof that when Mary Ann told me she had packed up bag and baggage to come to New York following her mother's death she was speaking the literal truth. On the Steinway was a silver-framed photograph of a pale, sad-faced woman who looked like Mary Ann quarter of a century on, and on a table alongside one of the armchairs was a Bible with a folded pair of rimless bifocals on top. While I stated my business, Mary Ann fixed me with that unwavering, glass-fronted, calculating stare. I went out of there wishing I had sent a telegram.

That was then; this was now. It was my turf, not hers, and she was the one who had sought the interview. There was no reason in the world why I should have to submit to being examined like a bug.

"At the risk of sounding ungracious, Mary Ann, I'm not feeling overly gregarious this morning. I assume you're here for a reason?"

"Yes." Nothing further was volunteered. The stare didn't change.

My irritation mounted. Crackerjack accompanist or no crackerjack accompanist, enough was enough. "Now look, Mary Ann—"

The doorbell rang. Deliverance. I got up with alacrity.

Mary Ann got up, too. "I realize I'm intruding, but Donnie Buell telephoned me a little while ago and asked me to be his accompanist for a performance of *The Sleeping Beauty* he's putting on. It's a little more complicated than the other times he's asked me to play for him because I'd have to put in a lot of rehearsal time and it would mean missing some of your classes. I told him it wouldn't be fair to you, but he said you know all about it and wouldn't mind and—"

"You thought you'd better check with me just in case there's a chance he might be shitting you."

"That's unfair!" Pink flooded her pale cheeks. "It's not that I doubt his word, it's simply a matter of courtesy."

"Of course it is. I was out of line. I'm sorry."

She wasn't appeased. The color didn't leave her face and her eyes defied me to say anything against Donnie. Odd that she should be his champion, given the rigidity of her outlook, her intolerance for life-styles that diverge from the straight and narrow. Some frustrated maternal instinct? Or could his religious fervor be the attraction?

The doorbell rang again. I didn't drag my heels getting down the stairs. "If you want to lend Donnie a hand, it's fine with me," I threw over my shoulder. "In fact, I'd take it as a favor. He's inclined to be morbid and he was close to Nina Langlander.

Throwing himself into a project like this would probably do him a world of good just now."

"I see. Well, in that case, I can scarcely refuse."

Little martyr. Of course she could refuse. Nobody was twisting her arm. I refrained from pointing that out. Sometimes I can resist temptation with the best.

My second visitor was even more of a surprise. Detective Sergeant Anthony Tagliaferro, large as life in jeans and an army fatigue jacket that looked as if it hailed from World War II and had been through every war since.

"Good morning, Ms. Tremayne. Got a few minutes?"

"A few."

"I see you've taken my security warning to heart. But I'd recommend getting a peephole. Saves wear and tear on the lungs and you'll be able to see what's on your doorstep." His hooded gaze moved from me to the stairs behind me. "Ms. Sanders, isn't it?"

"Yes. I was just leaving." Mary Ann walked briskly between Tagliaferro and me and let herself out. It occurred to me, as I bolted the door behind her, that she was probably the only person I knew who wouldn't find an excuse to linger on the chance of seeing me hauled off to the slammer. My ration of gallows humor for the day. I could afford to indulge because I was sure that Tagliaferro hadn't come to hassle me. Why I should have been sure I don't know, but I was.

"What did the mouse want?"

"To ask for some time off so she can take on another project."

"Sounds like the kind of thing the telephone was invented for. But maybe the perspective is different in Mouseland."

What business was it of his? Dedicated cop wanting to know about everything in his purview? I wondered about it for a moment—about all it was worth. I had more important things to wonder about. Such as why he was here.

He didn't enlighten me right away. Like Mary Ann, Tagliaferro appeared to be in no hurry to get down to business. Sitting down at the table in the chair he had designated his own, he accepted my offer of coffee and sipped in silence, the dark, sharp-featured countenance remote and forbidding. When at last he spoke, it was to remark that it was obvious I enjoyed teaching "one hell of a lot. Even I could tell what was happening in your studio the other day was pretty special."

"It was, but having a class take wing like that was a bit of a fluke. Usually my classes are workmanlike, no more. I'm not training any Suzanne Farrells or Gelsey Kirklands. Every ballet mother worth her salt knows the place for talented kids is the School of American Ballet. I get the leftovers."

"Apparently you can do a lot with leftovers. You have a very good reputation."

"I know I have. What I said sounded a lot more sour than I meant it to. Ballet's so big time nowadays the instruction has become pretty much institutionalized. On the whole that's a good thing, but it doesn't leave much room for independent teachers. Still, there are rewards. Like having a few SAB rejects study with me for a while and get taken into the school the next time they audition. Or monitoring the progress of singers and actors who take class with me to improve the way they move across a stage. You wouldn't believe how gratifying it can be to walk into a theater and see some quondam klutz you've taken on—But you didn't come all the way over here on a Sunday morning to discuss my pedagogical skills."

"No." He sighed. "I'll level with you, Ms. Tremayne. It can't be news to you that on paper you're our leading suspect. It's lucky for you your fingerprints weren't on the murder weapon. They weren't on any of the skewers we took from here either, which seems a little peculiar."

"Not really. I wear rubber gloves when I clean them, and I simply haven't used them since the last cleaning."

"Like I said, lucky for you. The other thing in your favor is that we haven't found anybody who disputes your statement that you and Nina Langlander were on good terms recently. A motive twenty years old is too much of a back number, even for a hard-nosed cop who likes to plump for the obvious."

"How disappointing for you."

He slammed his mug down on the table. Coffee spilled over the rim. He jumped up to get a handful of paper towels and mopped up vigorously. "Sorry about that. I'm afraid it's going to leave a stain."

"Just one of many. Improves the texture."

"Never at a loss for a comeback, are you?" He dumped the paper towels in the garbage can and sat down again. "I know it's hard, but do you think you can put a lid on it long enough to listen to what I have to say?"

"I'll try." I got up and took his mug to the coffee maker and filled it. Passing the peace pipe.

"Thanks. I want you to know this visit's strictly off the record. The hard-nosed cop I was referring to is my captain. If there were any evidence against you that a DA would be willing to take into court—" He shrugged.

I wanted to ask him why he was telling me this. I bit my tongue instead.

"Since the last time I talked to you we picked up a rumor that Nina Langlander planned to write her memoirs. Ring any bells with you?"

"Well, every now and again she'd say something like, 'One of these days I'm going to get in touch with Jackie Onassis and tell all.' But I never took it seriously."

"You and practically everybody else she knew, considering how long it took us to get a wind of it. So we asked that sister of hers whether there were any personal papers she kept outside the apartment, and you know what? Turns out she had a bank vault just for that—she seems to have been big on bank vaults. Sis was none too happy about turning over the key. Private stuff. None of our business."

"What was in the bank vault?"

"Ledgers and such. In case her accountant had a fire, I guess.

Plus a diary she'd been keeping since she was a teenager." His eyes bored into my face. *J'accuse.*

I picked up my mug and gave it a lot of attention. Guilty as charged. For of course I had known that Nina kept a diary, or at least that she had kept one years ago. I simply hadn't thought to mention it.

"What the hell goes on in people's heads, I wonder? Anyhow, we've got the thing now. I've turned all the pages. Compiled a list of suspects a mile long. Set the troops to checking alibis. Not that alibis mean squat. The league she traveled in, buying a hit would be a piece of cake. There's a major problem with the hit hypothesis, though. The skewer. A pro doesn't mess with found weapons, he brings his own. Unless it's part of the contract to finger somebody else. Pro or amateur, whoever it was sure as hell tried to finger you for it. Damn good thing you found that jewelry and had enough nous to get rid of it before we came looking."

I froze. "I don't know what you're talking about."

"Balls, Maggie, don't waste your breath." Tagliaferro leaned across the table and took the mug out of my hand and put it down out of my reach. "I think the table's been improved enough for one day, don't you?"

I let out a sigh almost deep enough to blow the house down. "All right. I did find the jewelry. By accident. Or luck. Or—"

"Better you don't tell me. Officially, we got an anonymous tip that didn't pan out. Mailing the jewelry to Sis was a blunder. You should have dropped it in a trash can or hidden it."

"But—"

"I know. You didn't want the killer to get off scot-free while we chased our tails looking for a mugger."

"You must think I'm an absolute cretin."

"No, just distraught. At least you had the sense to make sure we couldn't trace the package—about the only thing you did right. I can't prove you sent it, and I didn't come here to browbeat a confession out of you."

"Why are you here?" Even as I asked, I felt a knot forming at the pit of my stomach. Whatever was coming had to be bad.

"We could both use a refill." He got up, took both mugs to the coffee maker and filled them, came back, sat down. A major league stall.

The knot became a stone. "Well?"

Tagliaferro shrugged. "I've got a bad feeling about all this. The attempts to implicate you might just be diversionary tactics, but they might be something worse. That skewer really bothers me. Lifting it during the party would have been risky as hell. Assume it wasn't lifted at the party. Assume it was lifted ahead of time. Throw in planting the jewelry on you and tipping us off about it and we're talking pretty heavy calculation. Too heavy for dropping a scent of red herring."

I took a deep breath. "What are you trying to tell me?"

"That whoever iced Nina Langlander might be out to get you, too, one way or another. I think it might be a good idea if you watched your step for a while. Take a few elementary precautions. Make sure the building's clear during breaks between morning and afternoon classes and keep the front door locked. Have your visitors come in groups. If somebody wants to go one on one, make sure it's in a public place. Don't accept any packages you're not expecting and throw away all the junk mail."

I stared at him. "You can't be serious."

"I'm serious." He leaned forward, the swarthy warrior chief's face anything but wooden now. "Don't make the mistake of dismissing this as a gambit to make you think you're no longer under suspicion. You're still at the top of the list. If any hard evidence against you turns up, I'll have to run with it. But I happen to think you have worse things to worry about. Mind you, I could be wrong. It wouldn't be the first time."

I didn't say anything. He had succeeded in transmitting his bad feeling to me—and then some.

And here I'd been feeling almost cocky because I'd been so sure he hadn't come to arrest me.

"There's another reason I'm here. Also unofficial. Nina Lang-lander's diary. I got as much out of it as I could, but you know better than I do how closed the dance scene is, so I probably missed things. What I'd like is for you to come down to the office and go through the diary for me, see if you can pick up on anything that might get by an outsider."

I wondered if he had scared the hell out of me in order to persuade me to do his work for him. How comforting it would have been to believe that.

"I know it's asking a lot, Maggie. Reading that diary's going to be painful for you, no question. Chances are nothing will come of it, but you have the right mind set and you knew her better than most, so I think it's worth a try. Up to you."

Nonsensical to make it sound as if I had a choice. Though painful wasn't the word to describe what reading Nina's diary would be for me, I had to do it. "All right. When would you like me to come in?"

"How about right now? I'm parked around the corner."

His car was an old Volvo, painted the shade of beige that always looks dusty, with brown pile upholstery worn smooth and a pervasive odor of tobacco, but it rode like a dream. What his office was like I never found out. He took me through dreary gray corridors to a gray box of a room with a wooden table like the kind I remembered from kindergarten, only bigger, and four slat-back chairs designed for maximum discomfort. He told me to have a seat, he'd be right back, and left me alone in the box. For a totally mindless instant I seized up, his assurances that he didn't regard me as a suspect notwithstanding. But he did come right back, carrying a cardboard carton. He set it down on the table and lifted out a stack of notebooks bound in dove gray leather embossed with stars. Though I had never seen the binding before, it shrieked of Nina. Heat rushed up to my eyes, and I was afraid they might overflow.

"It reads like a fairly typical diary till around a dozen years ago—what she was thinking and feeling about this, that, and the other. Maybe nothing that far back is relevant, but you never know. The more recent record reads like an expanded date calendar. Who, when, where, what. Data she could have drawn on for a kiss-and-tell bestseller or for blackmail. Don't bother to protest. We can't discount the possibility. She used initials a lot. In most cases ID's weren't a problem, but there are still a few blanks. I've queried them."

I glanced at the abundance of yellow paper tags sticking out of the notebooks. "It looks as if 'few' falls a bit short."

"Double-checking, for the most part. I'm afraid you'll have to read in here with the door locked from the outside. Sorry about that, but the diary's evidence. So if you need to make a pit stop, better do it now."

I said I was ready to start, and he showed me the buzzer to press when I wanted him and left me. I don't know how long I sat with the stack of silvery leather volumes that enclosed so much of Nina's life in front of me, unable to bring myself to touch them. Merely looking at them was almost too much to bear. But there was nothing else to look at except the dingy room. Gray walls, gray door, gray metal grill on the window, gray linoleum on the floor. Even the wood of the table and chairs had a grayish tinge.

I forced myself to reach for the gray notebook on top of the stack. The earliest, if Tagliaferro had arranged them in sequence, and of course he had. I flipped through page after page of preoccupation with high energy–low calorie food regimes, methods of treating blisters and calluses, and the like, interlarded with bumptious judgments of the ballet establishment—exactly the sort of stuff my teenage diary might have contained, if I'd kept one. The second notebook was more of the same. I tried the third and opened to a date when Nina and I were sharing the apartment on West 111th Street. At once memory conjured up the smell of the place, the dancer's mélange of Johnson's Baby Powder and Pour le Bain, overlaid with Bellodgia, Nina's favorite perfume; conjured up an image of Nina in a mauve silk kimono sitting at the splintery pine kitchen table and chewing on the end of her pen, a black-and-white speckled notebook open in front of her (the fancy binding had been added later). I remembered how she used to leave the notebook lying about, trusting me not to snoop or perhaps not caring whether I did or not.

How was I going to be able to handle this? How?

I put the notebook down. Picked up the next. Steeled myself and opened it a few pages in.

> . . . shoes buckled on stage. Telephoned Selva this morning and a prissy little miss spouted some mumbo-jumbo. I'll deal with them tomorrow in the flesh. With a hatchet or a shotgun, if necessary.

I flipped a few pages.

> Visitors during intermission—horrid custom. Especially when they're Mrs. Big Tits. She's Lady Booby to the life, only her thing is cultural voyeurism, not sex. Far less healthy—and boring to boot.

I had to smile. I remembered Mrs. Big Tits, a good-hearted matron from East Hampton, long deceased, who fancied herself another Misia Sert. Well, maybe everything wasn't going to be painful. I flipped to the last few pages of the notebook.

November 16, 1966   *New Orleans*

> Forgot to draw curtains and woke up to view of wrought-iron scrollwork of balcony. Lovely against morning sky. Whole city lovely, when you can see it. Misty most of the time. Yet every day French Quarter crammed with easels, people behind them daubing away as if possessed. From memory, perhaps. Place is supposed to be the Paris of the South. Puffery, except where cuisine is concerned. That

really is superb. Last night I was ticked off when Thorenstein took us to a watering hole on the bayou—assumed he thought we weren't big time enough to rate Antoine's or Galatoire's. Not so. Food turned out to be fabulous. Doubt if I'll taste better shrimp in hot sauce if I live to be a hundred. Tried to negotiate with waiter for recipe, but kitchen security too tight. Don't blame them. Thorenstein pleased as punch to see us pig out.

To do the man justice, he went out of his way for us. Apartment instead of hotel room. Limousine. Integration still makes everybody uncomfortable here, not just types who think it's a fighting word. Maggie took a bus ride and made a point of sitting next to a black woman; drew withering stares and made the poor soul twitch in misery. T's personally seeing to it Allie doesn't have any confrontations—with maximum tact and minimum fuss. A real gent. Rara avis on management scene. Or any other.

Performance went like a dream. Advance peep at audience not reassuring. Very integrated, very self-conscious. Thought it would take howitzer to get rise out of them. Not so. Allie's *Dying Swan* had them in stitches, and when we got to the *Pas de Quatre* they were stomping in the aisles.

Resolved: Next time round get somebody to take me to Antoine's.

I closed the notebook. My memory cast up the wrinkled, scared face of the old black woman on the bus, still vivid after all these years, and my eyelids started to prickle.

Oh God. How was I going to cope with the upcoming crunch?

Anticipating trauma wouldn't help. I reached for the next notebook.

April 23, 1967   Los Angeles

Not my town, never will be. Whose then? Nobody of flesh and blood, that's for sure. Except tourists. Allie and

Karin did the gawk tour. Even Maggie, who's been along the Yellow Brick Road to Tinseltown before, wasn't averse to doing Disneyland. Which left the ferret-faced banker from Eagle Rock to me. I had to endure a visit to the poor stage-struck goop's private museum of ballet memorabilia (en route we passed a mural of smiling man and two small boys with caption saying Dad serves you today, sons tomorrow—too much!) but happily we stopped at Van Cleef and Arpels first. Remarkable how a sapphire pendant helps take the edge off boredom.

Disneyland must have cast quite a spell, or maybe it was the spirit of Mabel Normand or Carole Lombard hovering overhead. Karin, normally the most phlegmatic of individuals (if Balanchine had made *Four Temperaments* on her it might be a different ballet) was positively the most hyper sylphide in living memory. Allie's mode of cutting up was to turn her adagio into a temptress number to end all temptress numbers—sort of Lileth and Lamia, Ida Rubenstein and Theda Bara rolled into one. As for Maggie, her rendition of the kind of self-absorbed cavalier who either drops his partner or lets her wobble, wobble like a weather vane was just about perfect. I had to match her, and when she signaled that she was about to let go, I fell with spectacular abandon. Her phony solicitude was masterly, and of course we were at daggers drawn for the rest of the pas de deux. The audience went wild. Doubtless most of them thought what they were seeing happens every night. Little do they know. However hard you work—and most dancers work their tails off—the transfusion from the cosmos that sends a performance into orbit is a very sometime thing. Probably just as well. If I tried to negotiate that fall every night I'd likely as not be a mass of broken bones.

I put down the notebook and walked to the window; looked out at a concrete facade studded with mean little windows wearing grilled veils. I was approaching the big hurdle, and I wasn't ready for it. But then, no way in the world I ever could be ready for it. I returned to my chair and turned more pages.

September 7, 1967   New York

Getting used to my own bed again. A real acclimation project—seems as if we've been on the road forever.

Double performance yesterday. Terry recruited entire *Pas de Quatre* for private charade. Not the kind of thing we'd get roped into as a rule, but Terry's our musical guru and where would we be without him? He's in a bad way over Donnie, poor soul. Game enough, I'll give him that. Amused by the giddy butterfly antics and doesn't seem to be put too far off stride by Donnie's incurable fickleness. Problem is he's married, with toddler to boot. Wifey doesn't know the "somebody else" is a man and he's afraid she'll be crushed if she finds out. Brought her to Mrs. Big Tits's pre-performance garden party. Little Mrs. Woebegone to the life. Permed mousy blond hair, neat little straw hat, white gloves. Sat in a wicker chair still as a sphinx and watched the four of us crawl all over her husband and pretend to eat him alive with no expression at all on her pinched little face. The idea was to conceal the guilty party so nobody would be singled out for tears and recriminations (our Terry is scrupulous to a fault). She bought the act hook, line, and sinker and thinks hubby's running a harem.

As if it matters. When you're dumped, you're dumped. What's the difference whether it's for a woman, a man, or a string of ponies? Terry's hoping she'll give up on him eventually and scoot on back home to the boonies, but so far she's hanging on like a barnacle. Ah well, another day, another tiny drama.

Only yesterday afternoon I had been looking at the picture of that harem. Creepy to think about, like a kind of backwards clairvoyance. I felt as if I were somewhere out of my body, looking in two directions at once.

But I wouldn't be far enough out of my body for what was coming. Not possibly. I turned pages quickly. Now or never.

January 30, 1968   New York

What a homecoming. We were like a funeral cortege at the airport. Maggie the corpse, lying so white and still on the stretcher. A short flight, but it seemed as if we were airborne half a lifetime. Spent it huddled round the bed they'd set up for her, making a show of protectiveness. As if we could protect her from anything. She wouldn't speak to us, wouldn't even look at us, just stared straight up. And those eyes! Tar pits, with the skin around them raw and flaking, like scorched desert earth. No doubt she shed every tear she had in her in the hospital last night.

Damn, damn, damn! It could have been any one of us. Why didn't we refuse to go on when we saw that floor? Why isn't there a law against booking dance performances in halls where the stage is a layer of boards over concrete? Because then lots of dance performances might not take place at all, I suppose. We complained, of course. Fat lot of good that did. Comeback was a glib recitation of how many dancers had been before us. Probably most of them complained, too.

I couldn't sleep for replaying that moment in my mind. That ghastly, never-to-be-forgotten moment when Maggie soared in cabriole and came down and her leg buckled under her and she dropped as if she'd been shot. A sight you hope and pray you'll never have to see. Reports of disaster are agony enough—when I found out about Tanaquil LeClercq's paralysis I couldn't eat for a week. This was Maggie, my friend, who had been in my arms only moments before. We all knew it was bad. Helped her into the wings without a word and left her there. Went back on stage to finish performance. Show must go on, God knows why.

It's her knee. The worst possible injury for a dancer. The local quacks said "ligament damage" and fell all over themselves to ship her back to New York to find her own miracle man.

Only there aren't any miracles. If she's torn up those ligaments, that knee will never be the same.

I'm sure she's torn them up.

Poor Maggie. Junior met the flight looking as if he'd just tossed his cookies. What she needs is a rock, and he's a reed. Not bamboo either. The kind that bends with the wind but breaks anyway. He won't be able to handle this. He'll withdraw by inches and her heart will wither and crumble to dust.

February 30

Talked to Dr. Fitzgibbon. Maggie's injury bad as bad can be. She has. . . .

I snapped the notebook shut. I didn't need to read Nina's recapitulation of the diagnosis I knew by heart.

My eyes felt scalded and there was a knot in the pit of my stomach. But I'd looked into the abyss, faced the worst. Now I could begin at the first page of the first notebook and go straight through to the end.

There were no real surprises. The part of the diary that truly was a diary went up to the middle of Nina's run as second lead in *Roman Fever*, the musical version of *Daisy Miller*, which had put her legs on the advertising map. It was wry, often funny, often bitchy—evocative to anybody who knew the ballet scene. The thought occurred to me that if you put it into a time capsule, nobody pulling it out a hundred years hence would get much of a sense that the era covered was the era of Vietnam, peace marches, Women's Lib, sit-ins, flower children. Typical dancer's myopia.

The rest was what Tagliaferro said it was, a record as dispassionate as a calendar. Names or initials, dates, events, social and sexual encounters, tidbits of gossip were set down like notes to be worked up into something—or nothing. The record came to an end in the middle of the last volume, at about the time the relationship with Robbie became serious. Nina and I had been estranged over some of this stretch, so I couldn't identify everybody. Still, I could make educated guesses, and when I finished reading most of the blanks were filled. For whatever that was worth.

I pressed the buzzer, and a moment later Tagliaferro came in. He sat down and took a pack of Pall Malls out of his pocket and asked if I was "one of those antinicotine fanatics." I said I wasn't, I'd even been known to indulge on occasion. He shook out a couple of cigarettes, handed me one, lit it for me. I drew the first unfiltered puff I'd had in too many moons to count. It felt like sandpaper rasping down my throat, up to my nostrils.

Then, suddenly, I was crying. Great gulping sobs gushed up from nowhere and simply erupted. "I'm . . . I'm sorry," I gasped. "This is shameful."

"There's nothing to be ashamed of."

"The hell there isn't." I swallowed hard. Once. Twice. Three times. The crying jag was over. I drew on the cigarette again. "You see, a dancer's career is so brief, and to be robbed of even a minute of it—After I tore up my knee I went into a tailspin, wallowed in a morass of bitterness and self-pity. It didn't do any good to tell myself I was lucky, I could still lead a normal life. What's a normal life that doesn't include dancing? Anyway, it took me ages to pull out. Reading that diary plunged me right back in. That's why I was crying."

"You're entitled. Sorry I had to put you through it."

"I know. Look, if you're seriously considering blackmail I think you're wasting your time. Nina had plenty of money and some tried and true methods of getting more, and she wasn't interested in power. Besides, blackmailing people over what?

Rolls in the hay they think their spouses don't know about? Serving up coke at parties? Having the hots for young girls or young boys? Maybe I'm jaded, but that wealth of scandalous detail in the later volumes reads like notes compiled with an eye on the best-seller list. I mean, so what if she did write her memoirs? It's not a motive for murder. Gelsey Kirkland's still walking around, isn't she?"

"The problem is, you never know how people are going to react. Some straight-arrow type might get in a sweat over having a spotlight turned on his quirkier habits, so 'memoirs' might be a dirty word to him. Could be something like that." Tagliaferro shrugged. "I'd like it a helluva lot better if she'd written about how Larry Sondergaard collects gambling debts. Or how somebody got caught robbing the state treasury or passing the plans for a top-secret missile to Iran before the government could sell them. Like you say, these penny ante peccadillos don't seem like anything to get excited about. What about the earlier volumes? Anything jump out at you?"

"No. You don't seriously believe it could be anything that far back, do you?"

"It's reaching a bit, but Buell told us Nina Langlander had been uncharacteristically curious about the past recently."

"I know he did. He didn't think you paid it any attention. I guess he underestimated you."

"Just being thorough. We have to turn over all the rocks and pebbles. A grievance from way back when you and Nina Langlander were buddies could explain why the killer's been busting his butt to involve you."

"You're really committed to that hunch of yours, aren't you?"

"I'm not committed to anything. Like I told you, I've been wrong before." He took a deep drag on his cigarette and exhaled slowly. "Murders aren't very complicated as a rule. You look in the obvious places for a motive, and usually you find it. Not here. The robbery looked phony from the start. All the dough goes to a daughter whose great-grandma left her enough to start her own ballet company and make herself a star if she wanted to, so I can't see her doing Mom in for the inheritance. Maybe an old boyfriend took belated exception to being used, but it doesn't seem too likely. Everybody we've talked to agrees Nina Langlander was a bit of a bitch and a bit of a gold-digger, nothing excessive in either line, and she'd been behaving herself lately. When all the reasonable guesses seem to lead nowhere, you have to begin looking at the unreasonable ones and the possibility that the killer isn't operating with a full deck."

I didn't say anything to that. I couldn't.

"The past seems like a very long shot, I'll admit. The way she wrote about the *Pas de Quatre* days makes it sound like it was the best time of her life. Of all your lives maybe."

"It was." Strangely, saying it caused no pain. Maybe I'd reached saturation point. "You have to understand that the ballet scene is very structured. To get anywhere you have to be part of a company, and you know early on whether you have a future or not. That is, if you have any sense of reality—which, I'll concede, a lot of dancers don't. As I told you, Nina spent enough time in the corps at NYCB to know she wouldn't get much higher. Karin Holmquist was with the Metropolitan Opera Ballet—steady but not stimulating. I was too tall to get into a company corps and Allie Joyce was too black, so we were both working the fringe scene—Broadway, cabarets, television, whatever we could get. None of us had any illusions, so there was never any crap about sacrificing personal aspirations to the common cause."

"Convenient. You told me the idea for the group came from Ms. Langlander. Did she pretty much run the show?"

"No. The choreographer has to be in charge or it's hopeless. But Donnie Buell's no autocrat. He was always flexible and receptive to other people's ideas. Nina had lots of ideas and so did I. The others not so many, but when either one of them did come up with something, as likely as not it was a blockbuster we were all only too happy to go along with. The atmosphere wasn't seething with jealousy and intrigue, if that's what you're getting at. Comedy really has to be a team effort. There just isn't any room for ego trips. You work till you get things right. Something is funny or it isn't, people laugh or they don't. I'm not saying there was perfect harmony. We argued a lot. Could be that eventually somebody's ego would have swelled too much, but there wasn't any eventually, as you know."

"I had to ask." Unexpectedly, he grinned. "The idea that ballet behind the scenes is a hotbed of intrigue comes from the movies. I had to sit through *The Turning Point* three times."

"Your ex-wife?"

"My daughter."

"How old?"

"Ten at the time."

"That sounds about right. When I was ten it was *The Red Shoes*."

"I saw that one, too. With my ex. I guess I've seen just about every ballet movie ever made. The only one I didn't sleep through was Russian. *Romeo and Juliet*. There's a bit in it where Juliet wraps some black cloth around herself and runs over the battlements like a bird getting ready for take-off. It made me see what all the fuss is about."

He had zeroed in on the moment I would trade just about every other moment of filmed ballet for, and yet you can find hordes of ballet lovers who will tell you that Ulanova was too old, too thick in the middle to be dancing Juliet. I tried to visualize Tagliaferro sitting in a theater among the kind of people who go to ballet films. It boggled the mind. Like trying to imagine a martian at Shea Stadium.

"Listen, Maggie." He leaned toward me and put a hand on my arm. "I hope to hell I'm wrong about whoever wasted Nina Langlander having his sights on you. Could be we got that tip about the jewelry because he thought the frame was so good he didn't want his handiwork ignored, and that'll be the end of it. But do yourself a favor. Be extra careful. If anything out of the way happens—no matter how trivial it seems—call me right away. Day or night. If you can't reach me, ask for Captain Hendrickson."

I promised I would, and he gave me a card with two phone numbers inked in below the official one. He said he couldn't drive me home because he had work to do, but he would have a car take me, cutting off my protest with a terse, "No public transport from now on." He escorted me out of the building and put me into a patrol car with two stolid-looking uniformed cops, instructing them to check my place out thoroughly. I thought again of my earlier certainty that I had nothing to worry about from him today. Well, he had shown me my mistake and then some.

The first thing I did when the patrolmen were gone (they followed instructions to the letter) was whip up a meal in the blender—yogurt, banana, shredded coconut, wheat germ, jigger of grapefruit juice—and chug-a-lug it. Then I went on a cleaning binge. I tackled the studio first, going through it like a tornado with duster and dry mop, applying lemon oil to the barre and the Steinway, vinegar water to the windows and the mirror. The activity left me panting a little but not enough, and I went upstairs and continued playing hausfrau. The few times the phone rang I paid no attention to it. By nine o'clock the place smelled the way you expect houses in *House Beautiful* to smell. I untaped my knee, took a shower, and fell into bed, hoping I was whacked enough not to dream.

Fond delusion. As if it's possible to be whacked enough to shut out the demons of the night when your waking hours have done such a swell job of inviting them. This particular nightmare was no stranger. In it I am onstage, dressed as a cavalier in spruce green velvet tunic and putty-colored tights and boots, dancing a bravura variation of leaps and spins that Nijinsky might have performed, Baryshnikov might have performed, but not me. Never me. I soar higher than high, and in the split second before I start to come down panic grips my gut, my chest, my throat, all of me, and I know it would be better if I never land. Much good the knowledge does me. I'm not a bird or a plane or Superman. I touch down, and the floorboard slides under me. My left leg bends as no leg is ever meant to bend. Pain shoots through me, searing bone and flesh and sinew. It doesn't go away. Any minute, I think, they'll shoot me with a needle, a gun, anything to put me out of my agony . . .

I woke up with my knee throbbing as if the fall had happened yesterday. Gradually the pain subsided to a dull ache. Business as usual.

I didn't try to go back to sleep. I sat up in bed, watching the blackness metamorphose slowly into gray on gray. When the first slivers of light pierced the shutters, I got up and opened them, went back to bed and watched the sun come up. It was a pale, washed out excuse for a sunrise.

It occurred to me that so far I hadn't given much thought to Tagliaferro's warning of danger. I suppose when you get it with both barrels one bullet is going to bite so deep you don't feel the other for a while. There's a lesson there somewhere, I think.

Chapter 8

Two bad nights in a row and a day that seemed interminable made me slow to pick up on the distress signals in my last class. When you feel like a disaster area, you tend to think you're projecting, not receiving. As soon as I turned it around, I had no trouble pinpointing the source—green-eyed, freckle-faced, ten-thumbed Bridget Foster. I snarled at her for hunching her shoulders and the signals subsided.

No, it isn't witchcraft, merely the power ballet teachers have to read their students. If the soul is a closed book, the curve of an arch or the angle of a heel can open the pages, a porte de bras reveal what's written on them. Don't ask me how this can be, it just is. Francine Marza, my first teacher, had the power, but I wasn't all that impressed, I suppose because kids expect adults to know everything. That it might be something to wonder at I realized the day I went to watch a schoolmate take class with the legendary Alexandra Fedorova Fokine. I had to wait outside her studio for a class to end, and from my position near the stairwell I could see into a studio on the floor below, where a redhead in a black mantilla and pink ballet slippers was belting out "Hernando's Hideaway," bouncing up on point to accent phrases. I was mesmerized, and it was hard to adjust to Fedorova, a fragile old lady who never got out of her chair (she demonstrated combinations with her hands). There was no pianist, and she hummed Chopin softly, stopping frequently to yell corrections. Her prime targets were blond triplets about my age (twelve), agile and energetic but without grace or rhythm. Anybody would have thought, from the way she lit into them, that they were fiends incarnate, not the trio of klutzes they appeared, and that night I dreamed of a witch with Fedorova's face bellowing "Hernando's Hideaway" while three black cats with blond human heads thumped their tails. By the time I got to Korovskaya, the power was something I took for granted. Even so, the prescience of that massive, black-turbaned woman could be awesome. I remember a girl in class named Caroline, a hardworking, not especially talented fourteen-year-old with a waifish air and a stammer. The studio resounded with, "Don't look in the mirror all the time, Caroline," and, "Not to flirt with the hands, Caroline." Mysterious, but I didn't doubt Korovskaya saw something I couldn't see. Eventually Caroline dropped out of class, and I forgot her until about a year later, when I ran into her, tarted up to the nines, coming out of a bar on Lexington Avenue with a trick on her arm.

I'm not in Korovskaya's league, but what I can read in the tilt of a head or the breath of a hand is nobody's business. For a time I tried to kid myself that I was merely prognosticating from the known in a logical fashion, but deep down I always knew better. The touchstone is Bridget. She first came to me at ten, towed by a mother who thought it would be "neat" to be "into ballet." For almost a year I let her take up space in my studio and pretended to take her seriously—all I could do against the big black pit I saw gaping for her. It wasn't enough. She stopped coming to class and didn't return until a few months ago, this time escorted by her father's new spouse, a bespectacled, tight-lipped ash blond who stayed only long enough to scrutinize my studio and all three of my heads. Ever since, Bridget has been attending class faithfully, neat and proper in her black long-sleeved leotard and tights. As before, she progresses not at all. As before, I light into her as if progress were a possibility, promising myself that one of these days I'll have a long talk with her.

Today wasn't going to be the day. I gave a shout into the dressing room to please get a move on, I was in a hurry, and got back, "Yes'm, Ms. Legree" in a falsetto squeak (Marcia Feldman). Bridget was the first one out, laden with the huge backpack that turns her into a snail on legs. She gave me a nervous twitch of a smile and raced down the stairs. The front door opened and closed, and when they were all gone I bolted the door behind them (so there, Sergeant Tagliaferro).

I went upstairs to shower and dress. I put on one of my favorite outfits, a beige wool challis smocked Russian blouse and taupe doeskin pants, and checked out the back view in the full-length mirror behind the bathroom door. The line of my spine and shoulders looked firm and straight and confident, the line of my neck and head still good, with streaks of silver swirling gracefully in the black of my chignon. The final touch was a hand-woven purple-brown mohair wrap coat (a gift from a former student who moved to Santa Fe, hung up her ballet slippers, and transferred her artistic talent to the loom), and I was ready and waiting when the taxi arrived. Despite the rush hour traffic, the ride to the East Side was fairly speedy, and I discovered I was ten minutes early, so I had the driver let me out a couple of blocks short of my destination.

On the dot of six I walked up the steps of the familiar brick townhouse dating from the gilded time when making a killing meant you could leave your mark on the Manhattan landscape. The bricks were a mellower russet than I remembered, and the black wrought-iron scrollwork fortifying the windows was new to me. The mahogany door didn't require fortification; there were three bolts behind it. No nameplate. A stranger would have a hard time finding the doorbell, but I was no stranger.

Forsythe opened the door. He eyeballed me out of fishbelly whites without a sign of recognition and gave me a minimal bow. Right in character. Forsythe has always been part of Junior's life. Sometimes I think he's the reason for many of Junior's problems. Other times I think Junior would have a lot more problems without him. There's more than one way of looking at practically anything. He stood aside to let me enter the handsome mahogany-paneled hall redolent of beeswax and lemon and said, "The study, madam," sketched another bow and became a statue. Which meant I wasn't going to get his inimitable turnkey escort. Compliment? Insult? Or perhaps he was simply taking things easier as a sop to the years—he had to have seen at least seventy of them.

Nobody was in the study. I wondered whether Junior had ducked into the john, where he always used to repair before crucial situations. While it didn't give me any pleasure to think that seeing me again might be causing a crisis now, it didn't cause me any pain either. I sat down to wait in one of the applewood armchairs upholstered in butterscotch leather. All was exactly as I remembered. Satiny fruitwood wall paneling, toning in with the chairs, and the eighteenth-century bird's-eye maple desk you have to see to believe. Floor-length natural tussah curtains you can gather up in one hand, for all their substance. A magnificent room. I always thought of it as an extension of Junior, spare and elegant and gracious, quality in every centimeter, even though I knew the room was his inheritance, not his creation.

Junior made his entrance, resplendent in a gray silk suit with a fine burgundy thread in the weave, white silk shirt, burgundy silk jacquard tie, cordovan shoes. "Lovely to see you, Maggie."

He came over to my chair, stooped to plant a kiss on my forehead (benediction for Leda after the great rush was over?), and sat down in the master version of my chair behind the desk. "You're looking well."

"So are you," I said, with more truth than politeness. His six-feet-three frame was still trim (I blush to recall how important his being taller than I seemed once upon a time, and of course his not having an extra ounce on him heaped up the brownie points, dancers being weight conscious to the point of anorexia and sometimes beyond). His hair was the rich, sunny gold of long ago, with no sign of frost. His face was etched with creases and fine wrinkles around the eyes and mouth, but that was all to the good—people unmarked by time lines always look as if they've been pickled.

"What's this in honor of, Maggie?"

Good old Junior. Never any beating about the bush. "I want to talk to you about Nina."

"Nina?" The dark amber eyes were clear and candid and guileless. "I should have thought her a subject you'd prefer not to think about."

"I can't not think about her, Junior. She was murdered in my studio. That makes me a leading suspect."

"And the police are harassing you? What a bore."

"'Bore' isn't exactly the word I would have chosen."

"No, of course not." A small placating smile, with virtually no exposure of teeth. "If they're really giving you a hard time I can make a few phone calls."

"I'd rather you didn't."

"Still reluctant to face up to the fact that clout makes the world go round?"

"I faced up to it long ago. Around the time I found out standing on my own two feet wasn't in order because they couldn't take the weight."

I had aimed at irony, but it came out with such heartfelt bitterness I wanted to crawl into the woodwork.

It embarrassed the hell out of Junior, too. He propped his elbows on the desk and made a tent of his fingers. A familiar stalling gesture. His hands were beautiful, long and sinewy, with tapering fingers—the most beautiful hands I'd ever seen, I told him once; the rejoinder had been that lots of vestigial appendages were beautiful.

Odd the things one remembers.

"You say you want to talk about Nina. Let me see if I can guess why. You're uncomfortable under the gun and you hope that by emulating Miss Marple or Cordelia Gray you might rustle up some more suspects and take some of the heat off. Am I right?"

I had to laugh. "Just about. Put a tad crudely, though."

"My apologies. I'm afraid I'm going to have to disappoint you, Maggie, but the police have been here ahead of you. They already know that on the night of the murder I was at an après-ski party up in Vermont and hugely visible. Not that that proves anything much. Anybody can put out a contract."

This time I kept a straight face. "Yes. Anybody can."

Junior gave me a wry smile, a curl of the lip that somehow missed being supercilious. "Then the question would seem to be why, wouldn't it? Whatever there was between Nina and me was over a long time ago. Almost as soon as it began, as a matter of fact."

"And to think that once upon a time you told me she meant everything to you." Again what was meant to be ironic came out bitter.

"For God's sake, Maggie, that was a lifetime ago! Can you seriously believe a torch has been burning all these years? Or perhaps you think because Nina walked out on me a desire for revenge has been festering in my soul?"

"No, of course not. I just—"

The telephone rang. Junior made a what-can-you-do gesture and picked up the receiver. The caller was his broker. Knowing of old how long the conversations with his broker could last, I leaned my head back against the soft leather of the chair and closed my eyes. Bad move. The memory of the last time I'd been in this room came back to me. On the day of my graduation from crutches, I had made a trembling, effortful entrance with the aid of a cane, and Junior had welcomed me with the news that he and Nina had something going.

Too painful. I forced my eyes open, and they lighted on the desk, on a cup and saucer and a plate holding large, flaky crumbs, almost certainly from a croissant, Junior's idea of gastronomical nirvana. That triggered my memory again . . .

"Have some nourishment. You must be famished after all that splay-footed leaping about." The voice came from behind me. A long arm reached over my shoulder and dangled a croissant wrapped in a paper napkin.

"I think you've mistaken me for someone else, but food's food. Thanks." I accepted the croissant without turning around and bit into it. The filling was ham and melted Gruyère and it tasted wonderful. You never knew about the food at charity bashes—either ambrosia or a cut below Horn and Hardart. Hunger had induced me to wash off my Harlequin makeup and change into a dress, thereby rendering myself invisible.

"No, I haven't. It's the way you move. Smooth and seamless, like water rippling. Reminds me of Beryl Grey."

I turned around then, and found I had to look up slightly at a face with quattrocento planes, hair like molten gold—he was the most gorgeous man I'd ever seen. But it wasn't love at first sight, more like second, after he smiled a sunny little boy's smile and bared faintly grayish, fragile-looking teeth, proof he was human after all. I took it for granted that he had been told who I was, that the bit about recognizing me was a load of codswallop like the Beryl Gray line. In this I was about as wrong as could be. If there's one thing Junior knows, it's dancers' bodies; he can pick any dancer he's seen once out of the pack at a glance . . .

Junior hung up and tented his fingers again. "Where were we?"

"You told me you and Nina were ancient history." But what did that mean, when I could summon up details of my own ancient history as vividly as if they dated from yesterday? The dress I wore the night I met Junior, a grape wool Claire McCardell popover, originally my mother's, the four-poster bed in the colonial bedroom upstairs and the way my heart fluttered when I woke up in the morning with Junior's arms encircling me like a life preserver.

"But you don't believe me."

"Why shouldn't I believe you? I'm not here to accuse you of anything, Junior. I'm trying to chase down links to other people and I thought you might be able to provide some."

"Can't help you there, I'm afraid. I won't deny I saw quite a bit of Nina over the years. We attended many of the same parties, fund-raisers, what have you—the world seems to get smaller as one grows older—and we exchanged chitchat, nothing more. Leave it to the police, Maggie. They're not at all bad at it, though I concede that concentrating on you is hardly a sign of brilliance."

"Thanks for the vote of confidence. I presume that's what it is."

Junior sighed. "Christ, Maggie. Grow up."

I felt my cheeks flaming. Ironic that I, the injured party, should always be on the defensive, but that's because I've never got over feeling guilty over having allowed him to pay me off. Yet the settlement had covered the medical expenses and purchased the studio and left enough for my brother Eric, the family financier, to parlay into a fairly comfortable life-style, and where would I be now without it?

What really rankles, I suppose, is that I let him assuage his conscience at the price of mine.

"You're right. Forget I said that, Junior. It was dumb."

"It's forgotten." He looked down at his tented fingers. "Did Nina ever tell you what happened between us?"

"No. Why should she have? It wasn't any of my business, then or now."

"On the contrary. It had quite a lot to do with you."

"Junior—"

"It's time you knew the truth. Maybe then we can both bury it. I imagine you've always assumed that Nina betrayed you because I was a prize she couldn't resist. So did I, at the time. Later, I came to realize that she wanted to pry me loose from you because she knew I was anything but a prize as far as you were concerned."

"Junior—"

"Hear me out, Maggie. I'm not saying it was pure altruism. We all know what store Nina set by the obligatory tokens of courtship, and she ran true to form with me." The edge in his voice could have cut paper. "When Dr. Fitzgibbon told me about the pin in your knee, I almost passed out, and then I had to sit through visiting hours faking good cheer because nobody thought it was safe to tell you yet. Nina helped me through it, and afterwards she offered me a shoulder to cry on. That's how it started. She was a very quick study with people. I think she understood how appalled I was, how deeply it hit me, before I understood it myself. What I'm trying to say is that she provided a convenient excuse for me to abandon you. Which is what I would have done anyway, only it would have taken longer and I daresay hurt you far more."

("*He'll withdraw by inches,*" Nina had written in her diary. Here was confirmation from the horse's mouth. As if I needed confirmation. Yesterday, reading Nina's words, I had accepted them readily. Which probably meant that at some level below consciousness I had known all along.)

"If you're skeptical, I can't say that I blame you. The ink was barely dry on our divorce papers when Nina called the whole thing off. She said she was leaving before she got her first wrinkle and I walked out on her. Needless to say I was furious. However, over the years I've come to give her credit—albeit grudgingly—for sound judgment." His lip curled in the wry smile. "That would seem to be your cue to implore me not to be so hard on myself."

"Who, me? I'm the one with reason to be harder on you than you would ever dream of being on yourself. Remember? But since you mention it, it does sound as if you've developed a masochistic streak a yard wide."

"The psychobabble term is self-awareness, Maggie. Lest you think I spend my time contemplating my navel, let me assure you that I usually bend over backwards to avoid it. I said adieu to my psychiatrist years ago. Believe me, I wouldn't have trotted out that squalid squib of self-exposure for anybody but you. God knows I owe you that much."

"You don't owe me anything, Junior. I apologize for making you rake it all up, but there's a good reason. You see—" I took a deep breath, revving up to tell him about Tagliaferro's bad feeling and how important it had seemed to ascertain that if there was someone who had it in for both Nina and me, that someone wasn't Junior.

"I don't need to hear reasons." A smile came with that. The sunny little boy's smile I thought I would never see again. My heart skipped a couple of beats as a score of years were peeled away. The impulse to justify myself was stillborn. I couldn't bear to make the smile disappear.

Outside in the hall, someone was waiting, a tall, slender girl with a dancer's carriage, translucent skin, and a Psyche knot of rich auburn hair, tapping her foot and glaring at Forsythe, who barred her way in his most militant thou-shalt-not-pass manner. When I appeared, she transferred her glare to me. I wouldn't have been surprised to see her stick out her tongue—she was young enough for it.

Forsythe stepped aside to let her pass, then ushered me to the front door. "Taxi, madam?"

"Yes. Thank you, Forsythe."

A taxi appeared from nowhere the instant Forsythe stepped into the street. He whisked the door open for me and stood at attention. I got in, and as he closed the door he murmured, "Nice to see you again, madam," so softly that I had to strain to catch it. An unlikely valediction from the ceremonious sod who used to spit his "madams" out between clenched teeth and never lost an opportunity to make me feel like an interloper. Maybe I had heard him wrong.

I felt raw inside. Old wounds had opened, and if they weren't literally bleeding, they were aching like the devil. I had what I'd come for, though. Never again would I entertain the notion— even for a moment—that Junior might have been responsible for Nina's death. Inconceivable that she or any other woman could have done anything to hurt him where he really lived, in a rarefied atmosphere teeming with leggy, limber girls, omnipresent objects of everlasting desire. He was like James, the hero of *La Sylphide*, who abandons his betrothed to pursue a lovely, elusive winged being; when a witch offers him a magic scarf to enfold the sylphide so she'll be his forever, the poor boob snatches at the chance, and of course her wings fall off and she dies and James lives mopily ever after. Not such a good analogy. Junior wouldn't be dumb enough to fall for the scarf bit. Or if he did, he wouldn't mope about it—he would be after another sylphide like a shot.

It hurt, God how it hurt. I tried to tell myself that it was better to find out that I no longer existed for Junior than to go on suspecting that there was the remotest chance he might be the one who was out to get me, but it still hurt. And why shouldn't it hurt? I had thought it was going to be forever. If only I hadn't fallen and trashed my knee. If only Nina hadn't been there to swoop down on him. If, if, if. All these years I had been treasuring those might-have-beens like pressed flowers in a Victorian album. High time to close that album for good.

The taxi stopped for a light on Columbus Avenue, and I saw Shelley Russell, long white-blond hair floating free and face like a sunbeam above the charcoal gloom of her coat, walking arm in arm with Dr. Milton Frankovich, my ground-floor tenant. I felt like jumping out of the taxi and rushing over to her and telling her it wouldn't last, it never lasts. But of course I didn't.

. . .

I woke up. Suddenly and completely. The luminous hands of the clock said ten after three. I sat bolt upright, listening hard, trying to make my entire body hear. Something must have awakened me. Usually once I drop off without a struggle I sleep like a log until my body clock says wake-up time. Before turning in, I had put the tape of the Bolshoi *Romeo and Juliet* in the VCR and gorged on Ulanova's crowning achievement, and I was gone the moment my head hit the pillow.

I heard the ticking of the clock. I heard my own breathing, harsh and ragged. Nothing out of the way.

The refrigerator kick-started, settled down to a gentle hum. Still nothing out of the way.

I didn't believe in nothing. I sat taut as a wire, waiting for that other shoe to drop.

A creak. A very familiar sound. The tread of the eleventh step coming up from the studio creaks just that way when you put your weight on it.

Somebody was coming up those stairs.

Impossible. I had put up the barricades for the night. Locked the lock and drawn the bolt. Unless somebody had broken in while I was out seeing Junior, hidden when I returned and played possum and—

Played possum for eight hours? How likely was that?

Damn Tagliaferro and his bad feeling. Because of him I had made a fool of myself with Junior, and now I was on the verge of panic.

But the stair tread had creaked.

No. *Something* had creaked. Maybe the refrigerator had developed a new voice. Maybe the sound had come from outside.

Find out. Nothing else for it, except curling up and pulling the covers over my head.

I swung my feet to the floor and into a pair of black ballet slippers recently retired from the classroom. I had to grope in the closet for my housecoat, a beige silk kimono that dates from the

Pas de Quatre's one and only visit to the Far East, a three-week swing through Manila, Tokyo, Bangkok, and Hong Kong; if I was going to meet my maker, I would do it in style. I realized I wasn't frightened anymore, I was angry. Which is, I suppose, being territorial with a vengeance.

I tiptoed down the spiral staircase from my sleeping loft. The moonlight filtering through the slats of the shutters didn't make my living space bright as day, but it was bright enough for searching without turning on any lights. One thing you can say for an open plan—there aren't many places to hide. I checked out the bathroom and the storage room. Nobody. I looked under tables, behind sofas and chairs, even upended cushions. I went into the kitchen area and searched there, opening cupboards as if it were a real possibility that my pots and pans had company. They didn't. I was alone in my apartment.

Nobody had come up the stairs, obviously. Now I had to make sure that nobody had gone down them.

Fear caught hold of me again, a vise gripping my gut. I took a deep breath, opened the door, and started down the stairs. I skipped the step with the creaking tread and got to the bottom without making a sound.

The studio was flooded with moonlight, icy and eerie, the stuff that turns bushes into bears. Here it transformed the piano into some kind of extraterrestrial craft with a shadow full of menace. Nothing in that moon-drenched space moved.

Yet I didn't feel really alone. I never do. A functioning dance studio is a community, inhabited even when empty by the spirit of dancers gone and dancers to come. Was what I was feeling now all that unusual? I couldn't honestly say that it was.

I checked out the dressing room and the john, not expecting to find anything, not finding anything.

Nobody was here but me. Whatever I'd heard, it couldn't have been anything human. All was well.

But my heart was hammering. The vise still had hold of my insides. Deep down I didn't really believe all was well.

I was about to leave when I saw the shadow under the visitors' bench move. A trick of the moonlight? Imagination?

I switched on the light. Saw what looked like a mount of olive drab under the bench, quivering.

"Come out of there. Right now."

The mound had convulsions. A blue-jeaned leg terminating in a sneaker came forth. An arm in a long-sleeved sweatshirt. A head with a sandy pony tail, freckles like bruises, eyes with thick rings of white around the green irises. Bridget Foster.

"You have some explaining to do, chickadee. Get up!"

She had a little trouble extricating herself from the sleeping bag, no doubt a routine part of the gear that swelled her back pack. *Semper paratus*. I'd been more right than I knew, likening her to a snail. Now she hung her head, shell-less and vulnerable.

"I didn't mean to wake you. I got hungry and went upstairs to get an apple and accidentally dropped it on the floor. It made an awful lot of noise. I'm sorry."

An apple. Something I wouldn't be likely to miss.

"This isn't the first time, is it?"

She shook her head without lifting it.

"Are you still hungry?"

Her head came up slowly, those green eyes at once surprised and beseeching. "Sort of."

"Come on then."

She went up the stairs ahead of me, soundless as a ghost except when she hit that eleventh step. I sat her down at the table with a glass of milk and fixed her a monster sandwich on French bread—ham, Jarlsberg, lettuce, tomato, alfalfa sprouts, sliced olives, mayonnaise, mustard. She attacked it as if she hadn't had a square meal for months.

"I'm still growing," she said with her mouth full.

I wondered how she had managed on other occasions. The odd apple or slice of bread wouldn't have been enough to hold her. Probably she carried provisions on her back along with the sleeping bag.

How many other occasions?

Bridget finished her snack, took her plate and glass to the sink, and washed them thoroughly. She shut off the tap and reached for the dish towel. "That was great. You're not mad at me, are you?"

"Not especially. Where do you hide?"

"The niche behind the stairs. When everybody's out of the studio, I come back up."

"It must be quite a strain, keeping so quiet. Not to mention boring."

"I do my homework and stuff. Read a lot. It stays light pretty late and I have a flashlight. I like it here. It's peaceful."

"Don't they worry about you at home?"

"I tell *him* I'm staying with her and I tell *her* I'm staying with him." She hung up the dish towel and tucked her hands under her armpits. "They don't check up. They could care less. Funny, isn't it? When they were getting the divorce they both knocked themselves out trying to prove how much they wanted me, so the judge split custody between them. Too bad they couldn't saw me in half."

It seemed to me that they had done a pretty good job of it, but of course I didn't say so. I told her I was too tired for any more palaver and she should be, too. She wanted to crawl back into the sleeping bag, but I wasn't having that. I took her up to the loft and put her in my bed, where she curled up into a ball and was sound asleep in seconds.

I was through with sleep for the night. I thought about that niche under the stairs I had never checked out, about other possible hiding places in the building, about how vulnerable I was if somebody really wanted to get at me.

But that wasn't the immediate problem. Bridget was. What was I going to do about her? I had to do something. It occurred to me that Thea Davidson's school in the Village might be a solution. If I could sell Bridget on the idea of a boarding school that would permit her to keep up the connection with me or the studio or whatever drew her here, her parents wouldn't be likely to object, from the sound of things. First, of course, I had to sell Thea. It was meddling, no two ways about it, but I couldn't just let Bridget slip back into the pit. I didn't know whether those long sleeves were covering up needle tracks or wrist slashes, but it had to be one or the other—unless it was both.

In the morning there wasn't much time for conversation. Bridget wolfed down two bowls of granola and milk and fruit, and I packed her off to school (literally—lunch for a small army went into the portable house). I did manage to find out that she saw a shrink once a week ("A nerd. He drinks Dr. Pepper, for God's sake, and you wouldn't believe that corn pone accent"), which didn't seem nearly often enough, given her situation. But what did I know? My brief stab at analysis, to help me adjust to living without dancing and without a husband, hardly qualified me as an authority (my shrink drank Perrier and had a Viennese accent and yes, I thought he was a nerd).

I cleaned up the kitchen and sat down by the telephone, all set to make my pitch to Thea. But before I had the chance the phone rang. It was Donnie Buell, calling to tell me, with tears in his voice, that he had broken his arm. I commiserated with him and asked if there was anything I could do to help.

"As a matter of fact, love, there is. You recall that *Sleeping Beauty* I'm getting up for the rock and bicycle chain set? Well, I'd planned on doing Carabosse myself, but the cast has to stay on at least a month and the performance is only a couple of weeks away, and I was wondering—"

"Forget it, Donnie."

"But Maggie love, I'm up the renowned creek of *merde* without a paddle. I don't know where else to turn."

"You'll find a way. I have great faith in you."

"How? I'm practically paralyzed. Falling off a motorcycle is no joke, you know."

"You don't have a motorcycle."

"I was riding pillion. The little slut said he could ride with

James Dean. Please, Maggie. Who ever heard of a one-armed Carabosse?"

"A one-legged Carabosse is hardly an improvement."

"You know very well it's primarily mime. Anything that taxes the leg too much I'll change. I promise. You can use a cane. A crutch. A walker. Whatever. It's not as if I'm asking the impossible. You know the role. I'll never forget what you made of it."

"That was a long time ago. I said no, Donnie. No means no."

Chapter 9

*N*on *stúpida, ma troppo magra e testàrda*," the white-haired waiter said to Sergeant Tagliaferro in a recitative undertone, thumping the plates of *trenette col pesto* down on the table.

Tagliaferro flushed and searched my face with his hawk's gaze to see if I understood Italian. I sniffed the aroma of basil appreciatively and picked up my fork, not letting on that I knew I'd just been tagged skinny and pigheaded. What the hell, at least the old man had given me credit for brains—after a fashion.

We went to work on the pasta. In response to the obligatory query, I assured Tagliaferro it was every bit as good as he promised it would be. The restaurant, a Sullivan Street basement with flagstone floor, whitewashed walls, and no tablecloths, was clearly a well-kept secret from the fashionable world; the patrons looked like people from the neighborhood. I wondered why Tagliaferro had been so insistent that we had to have our talk over dinner. Maybe he thought I might be developing claustrophobia and was trying to be kind. One thing I could be sure of—it wasn't a date.

He wouldn't allow anything but small talk over the pasta and the *osso buco*, which was every bit as good. I said so, and asked him how he had happened to discover the restaurant. He said he'd known about it for years—no answer at all. He asked me how I felt about appearing on a stage after all these years (I'd told him to pick me up at Donnie's studio instead of my own, and of course he'd wanted to know why), and I said it would hardly be like facing a crowd that had paid top dollar at the New York State Theatre. So we were even.

When the *zabaglione* he ordered without consulting me arrived, he got down to business. He said he was glad I hadn't reported any trouble to him, but had I been bothered at all by anybody or anything I'd thought too trivial to mention? I said no, unless you counted nearly managing to spook myself out of my wits. I told him how I'd found Bridget Foster and her sleeping bag in my studio in the middle of the night.

His face was a study. Whatever he had expected to hear from me, it wasn't that. "What the hell did she think she was playing at?"

"She wasn't playing, that's the problem. One of your classic split-home refugees. She seems to have withdrawn from everything but ballet class. God knows why. It's not ambition—she hasn't any talent. And yet ballet's the only scene in her life she can relate to."

"And you're the only person?"

"I guess. Scary, isn't it? I've dished off some of the responsibility to Thea Davidson, who's marvelous with girls like Bridget. She's already working on the parents to get Bridget transferred to her school—they won't stand a chance against her." I hesitated. "You know, finding Bridget that way—it really brought home to me how vulnerable I am. But I suppose that flash is one anybody in my situation would have."

"Yeah, well, about your situation." He looked down at his empty *zabaglione* glass. "There's no easy way to say this. The thing is, I haven't been able to come up with any evidence to support that hunch of mine, and you say nobody's made a move against you. Looks like I was wrong."

"Simple as that." Anger welled up in me. On the strength of his hunch I'd barricaded my doors, denied myself human contact, and made a prize jackass of myself with Junior. "A misdiagnosis, in other words. Like telling me I have six months to live and then saying whoops, sorry, I must have confused you with somebody else. Only you haven't said you're sorry, have you?"

He looked at me steadily. "No. I haven't."

"And you aren't about to, naturally. Why should you? Why should you care that you scared me half out of my mind for no reason? All in the day's work for you, I don't doubt." My voice was strident.

He took the onslaught without moving a muscle, without a flicker in his eyes. My words bounced off that stony surface and boomeranged back. I was being monstrously unfair. Putting me on my guard hadn't been an act of callousness. Just the opposite. Well, I'd had a long day. Classes sandwiched around private coaching of a singer who had a chance to sing *Salome* in the boonies if she brought her own veils and a dance to go with them, and then tackling Carabosse because I'd been weak-minded enough to give in to Donnie's pleading. Which was no excuse.

"I'm the one who ought to apologize," I said, almost squeezing the words out of my throat. "You didn't deserve that."

He nodded. More in resignation than in anger. "The *zabaglione*'s too good to waste. If you don't want to finish yours, I will."

"Here." I pushed the glass across the table. "It's wonderful, but I'm stuffed." I watched him dig in. Unforgivable of me, but I couldn't suppress a tiny wish that he'd choke.

He savoured every mouthful; put down the spoon with obvious

regret. "There's an up side to everything, Maggie. After a month of digging we've turned up so much dirt that even Captain Hendrickson had to admit you don't make such a hot suspect after all."

"Sounds as if the main thing you've accomplished so far is to raise a dust screen for me."

"That's close. Unfortunately."

"I shouldn't complain, should I? I know you could have leaned on me a lot harder than you did. I know I should feel grateful to you, but I can't. I guess I won't be able to until you find out who really killed Nina."

"If you're fishing for guarantees, you're wasting your time."

"What is that supposed to mean?"

"You know what it means. Face facts, Maggie. We've expended an inordinate amount of time and—"

"*Inordinate?*"

"—and manpower on this investigation and we're no closer to nailing anybody for the Langlander kill than we were when we started. Frankly, I don't know where else to look."

He was trying to tell me that the investigation was as good as over, that nobody would ever know who killed Nina. In a minute I would hear how understaffed and overworked the NYPD was, how there were limits to the effort that could be devoted to any one case, and on and on and on.

I didn't want to listen. I couldn't bear to listen. All the resentment and anger I'd managed to check earlier welled up again, and this time I went with the flow. I impugned his commitment and his work habits, went on from there to his intelligence and his character. He stood it as long as he could before retaliating. Most of his artillery was directed at my emotional maturity, but when things really heated up he called me a ballsbreaker (don't they always?).

All the while we kept our voices down, so that nobody could hear what we were saying. Which is not to say that nobody knew we were going at it. After we fired our last shots and Tagliaferro paid the bill (I said I wanted to pay my share, but the look I got from him dissuaded me from pressing the point) and we got up to leave, the old waiter caught my eye and shook his head reproachfully.

I got angry all over again. At the waiter, at Tagliaferro, at myself, at life in general.

Still, give me a bang over a whimper any day in the week.

Chapter 10

In the classroom, wooden
chairs with writing arms were nailed to the floor and there were
bars over the windows. The light coming down from the recessed
ceiling fixture, filtered through a grill, was bright enough to
point up the magic marker graffiti on the mud brown walls and
the engravings on the writing arms, some traditional bondings
and lots more obscenities. Bright enough, too, to give me a good
look at myself in the mirror of my makeup case. War paint is
something I've always taken seriously. Long ago Korovskaya told
me, "You can plaster on stage white and nobody will think of a
sylphide and your smile is what a sick child puts on for visitors,
so you must look strong, strong, strong," and I've never forgotten
it. Tonight I started with a neutral foundation, Leichner number
2, lightly powdered. Then I did my eyes, outlining with kohl,

shadowing lavishly with the violet-blue-green range of the spectrum, achieving something that suggested twin tunnels with unspeakable horrors in the depths. A touch of charcoal to hollow out my cheeks and beak my nose, and I was ready to scare the world. Marcos Paredos of Ballet Theater once told a television interviewer that it took him several hours to apply his Carabosse makeup, which was a major league production. I allowed forty-five minutes for my more primitive efforts and was finished in twenty. It must be like riding a bicycle.

Carabosse, in case you don't know, is a wicked fairy, the evil genius of *The Sleeping Beauty*. Left off the guest list for the royal christening through an oversight, she avenges the slight by inflicting a curse: the infant, Princess Aurora, will grow up to be beautiful and, at the moment of her greatest glory, will prick her finger with a spindle and die. The ultimate in overreaction, you might say. In the original 1890 production at the Maryinsky Theater in St. Petersburg, Carabosse was performed *en travesti* by Enrico Cecchetti; Paredos was one of a long line of male successors that includes Frederick Ashton and Robert Helpmann. But men don't have a monopoly on the role, which was performed by Carlotta Brianza, the first Princess Aurora, in Diaghilev's 1921 London production (the first in Western Europe; spectacular and financially ruinous), and in recent years Monica Mason has been a powerful and utterly riveting Carabosse. I wish I could claim that my interpretation made a tiny squiggle on the historical record, but the *Pas de Quatre*'s spoof of the ballet wasn't one of our more memorable efforts, probably because the target was too easy. Still, doubling Carabosse and the prince gave me plenty of latitude for clowning, and I had some happy memories.

They weren't much use to me now. I was feeling the trepidation anybody appearing on a stage for the first time in two decades is bound to feel, and when I couldn't bear waiting for my cue in solitude any longer, I dashed out of the classroom, almost knocking over a stagehand. He was black, tall and thin as a rake, with hair cropped to stubble and a pink scar slashing the left side of his face from ear to chin. Eyes that looked as if they had seen everything opened wide at the sight of me. Very likely the ensemble of makeup, hair teased out like a galvanized mop head, and electric blue jogging suit festooned with big black rubber beetles and spiders (from a "fun" shop and supposed to cling to anything, but I had to stitch them on) would have stopped King Kong in his tracks. Well, slowed him down for a beat or two anyway.

The muzzy sound of the piano Mary Ann Sanders was coaxing music from ushered me into the wings. In the middle of the stage stood the infant Aurora's cradle, surrounded by Cabbage Patch dolls, Pacmans, Walkmans, and other trendy trinkets. The second of the six good fairies was bestowing her christening gift, a pair of rabbits in a cage (fertility), rocking them gently as she bourréed around the cradle. I couldn't see the audience over the footlights. I couldn't hear them either, and that had to be a good sign—they were hardly a crowd to hold back catcalls out of politeness.

I watched till the fifth of the good fairies approached the cradle with an armload of books (wisdom), then went to mount my chariot. Perhaps chariot isn't quite the word. What we're talking about here is the chassis of a 1975 Corvette, stripped with a thoroughness that would do any street gang proud and painted a piebald blue-purple-black, mounted on wooden wheels, and propelled by a winch. My attendants, dressed as the traditional two-legged rats with long tails and skull masks, were in a huddle beside the chariot and seemed to be afflicted with a collective case of the jitters. Seeing me in full regalia perked them up a bit, and, as I got into the chariot, one of them gave me a high five, not getting it quite right, but then you wouldn't expect a kid from the posh Connecticut school where Donnie gives workshops to get it right. I was bolted in from outside (the door hardware had gone the way of the window glass, the seats, the steering wheel, the engine), and I crouched on the floor next to a tin bucket, holding on to it so it wouldn't rattle. I checked that the four glass vials taped above the door frame were secure and took a couple of deep breaths.

The piano thundered menace, and the chariot began to move. Bumpily. I thought "rag doll" and relaxed my muscles to go with the bumps. The chariot came to a stop. The bolt was drawn. The door swung open. Slowly—very slowly—I unfolded my right leg to full stretch (not easy when you're in a crouch), toe pointed in the air like a projectile, held the pose for a moment, and sprang out of the chariot. Hardly a leap to remind anybody of Nijinsky in *The Spectre of the Rose*, but I was gratified to hear a few gasps. I crooked a forefinger at Catalbutte, the forgetful twit of a majordomo who had left Carabosse off the guest list—in this production a disc jockey with a Rod Stewart wig, earphones, and a microphone around his neck—and he approached me, quaking. With my left hand gripping the window frame of the chariot for support, I thrust out my right leg in a fast développé. My toe connected with his chin. Or so it looked to the audience. Actually, I never touched him—contact could have meant terminal whiplash. He twisted in midair and fell face down. I mimicked his quaking, bent down, wrenched off his earphones and tossed them aside, wrenched off his wig and tossed it to my rats, who devoured it gleefully (the bit with the wig is a big moment in *The Sleeping Beauty*; you would no more omit it than you would omit putting out Gloucester's eyes in *King Lear*).

The stage belonged to me now. I stamped my foot. I beat my toe against my calf. I walked over to the cradle, stabbing the floor with every step. I circled the cradle with piqué turns. Came to a dead stop in front of it. Raised my right hand and pointed at the infant; rolled up my left sleeve, made the first and second fingers of my right hand into a *V* over a vein and jabbed my thumb between them. Brought my arms up to my head, then down quickly, and crossed them with clenched fists in front of my body—ballet language for "die." The parents of the infant, Queen Barbie and King Ken, approached me with outstretched imploring arms, but I put up a stop sign with my hand and they froze. I tossed my head back and bared my teeth in silent laughter. I did my floor-stabbing walk to the chariot, got in, and one of my rats stealthily slid the bolt. I took down one of the glass vials taped above the door frame and tossed it into the bucket. The glass shattered and a thick black cloud billowed out of the chariot. I broke another vial as the chariot began to move offstage. Some guy in the audience called out, "Way to go, bitch!" and there were shouts of approval. Whistles. Stomping. Applause. I was a smash.

The chariot stopped moving. The door opened and I got out. My rats, jittery no longer, congratulated me with enthusiasm and dashed away to change costumes. I didn't have much to change, so I stayed in the wings to watch the delayed presentation of the Lilac Fairy's gift: mitigation of the death sentence to a long sleep from which the princess will be awakened by the kiss of a prince. Tradition calls for a confrontation between Lilac and Carabosse, white magic pitted against black, but Donnie did away with it ("You'll make a stronger impact if you sweep in and out like an ill wind instead of hanging about gnashing your teeth while virtue does its stuff," he told me). What's a small liberty like that when the Lilac Fairy has been turned into a Madonna clone with purple hair, the fatal spindle into a hypodermic needle, and the prince into a doctor in a hospital emergency ward? To purists, of course, a production like this is sacrilege. After all, it was a performance of *The Sleeping Beauty* at the Maryinsky that left the eight-year-old Anna Pavlova "living in a dream" and set her compass; at another performance, George Balanchine made his stage debut, realized what ballet was all about, and never looked back. But how can you offer straight Petipa to an audience of juvenile pushers, muggers, and God knows what all else? Whatever you want to say about Donnie's adulteration, it was holding them.

Mary Ann thumped out the closing notes of the Prologue, and I dashed from the wings to the classroom I was using as a dressing room, in a hurry because the intermissions were short (the authorities at the facility didn't want their charges sitting idle for too long a stretch), and I didn't want to miss anything. I pulled a long, shapeless skirt over my jogging pants, wrapped a big shawl around my shoulders, picked up a bulging Big Brown Bag, and voilà! the wicked fairy was now a harmless-looking shopping bag lady, the better to tempt you to the needle, my dear. I was back in the wings when the piano started up again.

Donnie had set Act One, Princess Aurora's birthday celebration, on a suburban lawn and interpolated the wedding divertissements from Act Three between the Garland Waltz and the Rose Adagio. Something else to make Petipa and Tchaikovsky turn over in their graves, needless to say, but not at all a bad idea for an audience unlikely to sit quietly for more after they know how things turn out. The needle has to be carried by somebody, so why not set them wondering which of the weirdos strutting their stuff is Hotshot Mary in disguise? The Macho-Macho Stud or his bone-weary Go-Go Girl partner (Puss in Boots and the White Cat)? The Hillbilly Girl or the City Slicker (Little Red Riding Hood and the Wolf)? Either of the one-on-one basketball players (Hop O' My Thumb)? The Jet Setter or the High Roller (Bluebird Variations)? At rehearsals I hadn't been entirely convinced that it would all work, but right now the pudding was being gobbled up by an audience tough in every sense of the word.

My cue came. I shuffled onstage, stooped with the weight of my shopping bag. Above the sound of the piano, I heard a collective intake of breath. They *knew*. Shelley Russell, the princess, floating around the stage from partner to partner, didn't know a thing. She caught sight of the poor old crone and stopped dancing to put a gentle hand to her breast. Her heart was touched. Naturally. What kind of a princess would she be without that heart? The party guests conveniently cleared the way so she could chaîné a straight line to my side (Shelley is a wonderfully precise, secure turner). What could she do for me? she mimed. Food? Shelter? Clothing? She took a ring from her finger and held it out to me. I accepted it; mimed my desire to give her something in return. She nodded, understanding and respecting my feelings, poor tenderhearted sucker. Out from under the shawl came the needle, and wham! The princess dropped like a stone.

Pandemonium. Queen Barbie collapsed into the arms of King Ken. The stage pulsated with bodies, bouréeing, spinning, staggering, miming grief for all they were worth. I dropped my shopping bag, flung off my shawl, tore off my skirt, and lo and behold! Carabosse in her electric blue jogging suit. No surprise to the audience, but they clapped for me anyway. I tossed my head back and laughed. I raised my right leg and did a rapid batterie, triumphantly stabbing the air with my toe. I was right square on top of the world. Certainly on top of the poor wretches cowering on that stage. My chariot rolled onstage. I stabbed the air one more time and leaped inside. A few of the courtiers found the courage to rush at the chariot (one of them unobtrusively slid the bolt home). Beyond their reach, I laughed at their efforts. I tossed a smoke vial into the bucket, and a black cloud rose up and swelled out of the window. The chariot started to move into the wings. I broke another vial.

There was no warning. One moment smoke, the next flames were raging everywhere. If the Corvette had been less thoroughly gutted, it might have been all over with me. It nearly was anyway. My reactions were unbelievably slow. I froze, while my mind catalogued colors in the flames with almost clinical detachment. Red. Orange. Pink. Blue. Violet. Green. Yellow. Only when a tidal wave of heat engulfed me did the danger register. My vision blurred. Smoke entered my mouth and seared my throat, and at last I comprehended that I would asphyxiate if I didn't get out of that car. I flung myself at the door and pushed. Stupid—I was bolted in. Miraculously, there was time to regroup. The flames were all around me now, yet they didn't seem to be touching me: I might have been made of asbestos.

I dived at the window. It moved away from me. The entire

door moved away from me. My forearms were grabbed and pulled and I found myself flying through the air. I landed on all fours. A heavy cloth was thrown over me. It smelled of mildew. I was pummeled and pummeled and pummeled. I thought I would suffocate. The cloth came away. I gasped for air. Coughed. Saw a shadow flitting away from me. The grim reaper?

My vision cleared. Amazingly, the flames were still contained in the Corvette, as if they were digesting their meal before foraging for more. Not at all the greedy, all-devouring destruction I've been conditioned to expect by the movies, but of course there was no engine, no fuel tank, only chassis. Thank God. I found I was holding my breath.

The skinny stagehand with the scarred face ran past me, carrying a fire extinguisher. It looked so small, so inadequate. He couldn't possibly cope with the flames single-handed. I wanted to dash for a fire alarm, a telephone, something. I couldn't move. I couldn't even shout for help. All I could do was stand and watch that stagehand attempt the impossible.

Somehow he was doing it. Like John Wayne wielding a tommy gun against overwhelming odds, he was mowing down the enemy. The blaze shrank and shrank. To a campfire. To little tongues of flame lapping at the crumpled shell of the Corvette. To nothing. The stagehand kept on gunning, a warrior who couldn't bear for the battle to end.

At last he stopped. I heard piano and guitar playing the lullaby to which the Lilac Fairy puts everybody to sleep. The performance was sailing along as if nothing had happened. Without the ruined chassis in front of my eyes to prove I wasn't hallucinating, I might have wondered if anything really had happened. I breathed in further proof, a stench that touched off a fit of coughing.

"Man, you sure one lucky bitch," the stagehand said softly. He was at my side, fire extinguisher in hand, looking like an armed scarecrow.

Horror hit me like a blow. "My God, if you hadn't pulled me out of there—"

A growl rumbled deep in his throat. "Somebody 'round here don't like you much, that's for sure."

"But it was—"

The music stopped. People came rushing off the stage. All of a sudden there was a crowd around the burnt chassis.

"Jesus!"

"No wonder I thought I smelled smoke."

"You didn't smell anything, you were too busy trying to keep from falling flat on your face."

"You might have been killed, Maggie!"

Donnie raced into the wings, right arm aglitter in a silver lamé sling. He pulled up short, aghast. "This is unreal." He came up to me and embraced me with his good arm. "Are you all right?"

"Fine. I was lucky. The stagehand—"

"To hell with the stagehand, it's you I'm worried about." Donnie's arm tightened, almost squeezing the breath out of me.

People milled around, expressing shock and commiseration in hushed, sickroom-visiting tones. Out of the corner of my eye, I spotted my sinister-looking savior, hovering and watching. Then Shelley embraced me, filling my nostrils with the smell of drying sweat and stale Arpège. When she let go, my savior was gone and I caught sight of Mary Ann Sanders, gawking at me as if I were a fugitive from Dr. Frankenstein's lab.

I looked down at myself. My jogging suit had disintegrated into tatters and charcoal. No wonder everybody was oozing sympathy.

"Maybe you ought to be checked out," Donnie said. "Milton Frankovich is around somewhere. He ought to be able to tell whether all the parts are intact."

"I'm fine, really I am. The fire didn't lay a glove on the quintessential me."

"Well, love, the exterior isn't anything to brag about at the moment. What happened anyway? How did the thing start?"

"I'm not sure. I tossed a smoke bomb and suddenly there were flames all over the place. The vial—something must have been wrong with it."

Donnie glowered. "I'll throttle Roger, the irresponsible twit."

Somebody snickered, quickly smothering the sound. Roger, the pyrotechnician Donnie has worked with for years, stands six feet seven in his stocking feet. Even I was tempted to smile. I could feel the anxiety starting to dissipate. Everybody was sliding into a show-must-go-on mind-set.

A little push was in order. "You have to get back out there in about five minutes," I pointed out.

"Are you sure you're all right?" Donnie asked. Some of his concern, I didn't doubt, was over whether I could make it back onstage for my cameo appearance before the final curtain. But not all of it. I assured him I was fine, and he gave me a quick kiss and darted away. Amid a babble of sympathetic clucking, the crowd dispersed, and presently the only ones left in the vicinity were a couple of stagehands, neither one my savior, goggling at what was left of the Corvette.

In the privacy of the bleak classroom, I collapsed into a chair. My muscles felt like jelly. I discovered I was shivering. The terror I hadn't felt while the flames were raging all around me caught up with me now.

By all rights I should have been dead. Sheer luck I wasn't. The crappy jogging suit I had bought purely for color hadn't burned, it had just melted away. Well, they say sometimes a little luck is better than a wagonload of talent or brains or beauty.

I couldn't stop shivering. My brain went into a funk.

The piano brought me out of it, sounding the music for the prince and his courtiers, or to be more accurate, the young emergency room resident and a flock of hospital personnel and patients. Somehow I got myself out of the chair with its enveloping writing arm. I peeled off the remains of the jogging suit with care, the way you might peel an overripe banana. I spotted a burn on my left thigh through a hole in my pantyhose, and of course the moment I did it started to hurt. I put some

Albolene on it and made a loose bandage with the gauze and tape I never leave home without. I put on my street clothes, black cotton turtle-neck and olive drab corduroy pants, baggy and old and distinctly short on chic, but okay for Carabosse, and changed my ruined slippers for my spare pair. A glance in the mirror showed me a streak of ashy grime across my forehead and another on my chin. I didn't remove them, I blended them in. I was ready.

The music told me it was almost time for the Lilac Fairy to accost the tired prince-doctor on his way home and show him a vision of the sleeping Princess Aurora. I decided I wanted to watch that. I would have wanted to watch anything, do anything, rather than hang around that classroom and think about the close call I'd just had.

So naturally the first thing I set eyes on was a walking reminder: the stagehand who had pulled me out of the blaze. The pink slash of a scar looked downright scary, and there was a mean glint in his eye. I had an impulse to turn and run for cover. Then I noticed that he had a bandanna wrapped around each hand and was heartily ashamed of myself.

"That must be very painful. You should have it seen to by a doctor."

His eyes slid into neutral: Standard Operational Procedure with Whitey. "Don't want no fuss. Start fussin', the man start thinkin' maybe I be the one tried to burn you up."

"That's ridiculous. You saved my life. Anyway, it was an accident."

SOP went by the board. His eyes grew wide with disbelief. "You tryin' to shit me or yourself? Somebody stick a little nitro in one of them smoke bombs, try to blow you up for sure. You lucky be still walkin' around."

"I can't believe it was deliberate."

But I could, that was the trouble. That was why my brain had been taking evasive action. It started revving up now, full speed ahead. The Corvette had been standing in the wings all day.

Anybody could have found opportunity to substitute a vial of nitroglycerine for one of the vials of the harmless chemicals that create smoke on contact with air. Anybody.

Many of the people who had been at my house the night Nina died were here tonight.

"You lookin' green, bitch."

"I'm okay. Do you think it's possible somebody here decided to play a practical joke and—"

"No way. Anybody here get hold of nitro wouldn't go wastin' it on no jokes."

I couldn't argue with that. My brain started backing off again. I would put the whole thing on hold, come to grips with it later.

Would it be any easier later? How much later? A week? A month? A year?

"Hey, don't you go passin' out on me now!"

"I won't. I said I'm okay. Thanks to you. I can't thank you enough. If it hadn't been for you I'd be—" I couldn't finish.

"Compost." His grin was wicked.

I managed not to shudder. "Is there something I can do for you? Maybe if I told the director how you saved my life it might—"

"Don't you go makin' my life no tougher than it is."

"Well, maybe when you get out of here I could—"

"Be here a while. Offed my old lady." He glided past me. "So long, bitch. Look after yourself real good."

I stared at him with my mouth open. I couldn't believe I had just heard a confession of matricide.

Maybe he hadn't meant matricide. Maybe "old lady" meant girlfriend.

Why had he killed her?

Maybe he hadn't killed anybody. Maybe he was lying.

Why would he lie to me?

Why would anybody want to kill me?

That one slid in before I could slam on the brakes, stop the wheels from turning.

131

I went into the wings. The prince-doctor was already at Aurora's bedside, gazing at her with what was meant to be rapture but looked like idiocy from where I stood. Hokey. Unreal. I couldn't track with it. In a few minutes Mary Ann would sound my music, and I was supposed to rush on, threaten the young couple with all the body language at my command, and stagger off at an imperious wave of the Lilac Fairy's guitar. I would never be able to make it. Not in a million years.

But when I heard my cue, I got right out there to do my thing. Once a trouper, always a trouper.

Chapter 11

The night was grisly. Every time I closed my eyes, I was trapped in that conflagration again, trying to fight my way out. And then, suddenly, I was free, confronting the scarred, desolate face of my savior, hearing him say, "I offed my old lady."

Somebody had offed Nina. A given.

Somebody had tried to off me. No proof of that, of course, but the stagehand had said nitroglycerine, and a vial of nitroglycerine hadn't got into the Corvette by accident. No proof either that the somebodies were one and the same, but mind, instinct, every atom of my being said they were. Anybody at the performance last night could have switched vials. Donnie had invited the world. His world. Nina's world. My world.

"Whoever killed Ms. Langlander might be out to get you, too, one way or another."

Sergeant Tagliaferro's words. All too prophetic.

Call him any time, the man had said. I had been tempted to pick up the phone the minute I returned home from the performance, but it was late, he was probably asleep, and I didn't want to make him sorer at me than he was already. The danger was over. Telling about it could wait a few hours.

What I hadn't bargained for was that the wait would be so agonizing. Sleep was out of the question: my brain was in overdrive and I couldn't slow it down. I tried switching on the bedside lamp to keep the demons at bay, but dark or light made no difference to them. I got out of bed and went downstairs to collect a stack of books with a superabundance of pictures—Boris Kochno on Diaghilev, Merrill Ashley on Balanchine, Makarova, Baryshnikov, and Martins on themselves—and sat up in bed turning pages until first light poked through the shutters.

I got out of bed and went downstairs and started a pot of coffee going. I went into the bathroom to wash and tape my knee, taking my time. When the coffee was ready I poured some and sat down at the table and forced myself to sip slowly. On *Hill Street Blues*, the cops always got their briefing around seven, but I've been conditioned all my life to the idea that the normal workday begins at nine. I compromised. On the dot of eight I made the call.

"Homicide. Phillips."

"Sergeant Tagliaferro, please."

"Not here."

"Can I reach him at home?"

"Nope. He's in Seattle. Seminar on procedures."

A knot formed in my stomach. "When will he be back?"

"Tomorrow afternoon. If he doesn't make a detour to Disneyland. Somebody else do?"

I thought about my name leading Captain Hendrickson's short list of suspects in Nina's death and decided to wait. When I hung up, the click made me think of a lifeline being severed. Irrational. But what does panic have to do with reason?

I told myself that even if I had got hold of Tagliaferro, I wouldn't be much better off. What could he do?

Listen. He could listen to what I had to tell him about last night and believe, where somebody else might wonder if I'd lost my marbles. After all, he was the one who had planted the idea of danger in my mind. An idea he had stopped believing in, but last night's ride in that flaming chariot had made a believer of me.

Damn the man. Why wasn't he around when I needed him? What business did he have attending seminars when he should have been on the job?

I felt like bawling.

The telephone rang. I jumped about a foot; knocked my empty mug off the table; managed to rescue it just before it hit the floor. When I lifted the receiver, it fell out of my hand and onto the table. I held on second try. "Hello."

"Maggie." Donnie Buell's voice was fraught. "I just talked to Roger. He says it's absolutely impossible the stuff in the vials could have started a fire. But I kept at him until he admitted he has a couple of trainees in his lab. One of them might have made a mistake. The thing is, if you sue Roger—"

"I'm not going to sue Roger. Don't be ridiculous."

"—he can get himself off the hook by putting me on. I was the one who picked up the wretched smoke bombs and—"

"I said I wasn't going to sue."

"—carried them in my attaché case. Honestly, Maggie, if I have to go into a courtroom and—"

"*Shut up, Donnie!*"

He did, and I succeeded in calming him down. I hung up wishing I could do the same for myself. The phone immediately rang again. Anita Langlander, wanting to know if I was all right.

"Of course. Why shouldn't I be?" Waspish. I tried again. "I

suppose you're all agog for details of the barbecue that almost was." The lightness that should have been in my tone wasn't.

"I can do nicely without them, thank you very much."

"Sorry, Anita, I guess I'm still edgy."

"It would be a miracle if you weren't. Maggie, I know it's early, but I couldn't sleep and . . . A couple of days ago I was going through Nina's things and . . . After what happened last night I thought—" She took in air with a gulp. "We have to talk. Right away."

What could have set off unflappable Anita? She had appeared perfectly under control last night. "My first class this morning isn't till ten. If you want to come over—"

"I can't. I'm expecting the charity people to pick up Nina's things. Could you come here? It won't take long, I promise. I wouldn't ask if it weren't important, believe me."

"I know you wouldn't. Twenty minutes."

It was slightly more than that. Anita was waiting at the open door when I got off the elevator and greeted me with an ardent hug.

"Thanks for coming, Maggie. Ignore the mess." She waved a hand at the stacks of cartons in the foyer. "All this is going to an outfit that holds auctions to help the homeless. I've had the devil's own time bringing myself to get it together, and now I can't wait for it to be out of here."

She led me away from the clothes, trinkets, and the rest of the portable fallout of a life, and I followed her down the marble hall. My heart sank as I realized we were headed for the room at the end. Nina's room. As always, it was redolent of Bellodgia, although the bottles of scent were gone from the whitewood dressing table with the alabaster top. Gone as well were the ivory and silver toilet articles, the only thing remaining the three-way mirror with the chased silver frame. Curtains of mauve silk (Nina was into pinks and purples for redheads when fashion still dictated blues and greens) were open on blue sky, which wasn't unusual, and on empty closets, which was. The bed, with its headboard like a huge mother-of-pearl fan, looked oddly desolate, and it took me a moment to figure out this was because Paquita, the oversized flamenco doll, was missing from her place on the iridescent oyster silk coverlet. Even without Paquita, even without so many of Nina's possessions, the room was heartstoppingly full of her. The ambiance was more than the scent, the subtle harmony of ivory and silver and mauve, the sum of all the remaining parts. To get rid of it completely, you would probably have to strip the room down to the plaster.

"Take a look on the nightstand," Anita said in a small, tight voice. "The envelope. I found it in the drawer under some travel brochures." She backed up against the door frame, distancing herself.

The envelope was the only thing on the marquetry top of the nightstand. I went over and looked at it, a perfectly ordinary nine-by-twelve manila envelope, addressed to Nina in block capitals, postmarked New York, N.Y., December 12 of last year. I picked it up. It didn't explode, burn my fingers, anything like that. I opened it. Inside were some thick pieces of paper with neatly torn edges. A trashed poster of the *Pas de Quatre*.

I felt the hackles rise along my spine. I knew now why Nina had paid that visit to Donnie and pumped him about enemies the group might have had.

"The police made a thorough search," Anita said. "They must have overlooked it. Or maybe they found it and didn't think it meant anything. Maybe it doesn't but . . . I didn't discover it until a couple of days ago, and it gave me the worst vibes because . . . There's something you don't know. Nobody does—the police asked me to keep it to myself. I had no problem with that. But now . . . I got a package in the mail. Nina's ring and watch and the pendant she was wearing the night she was—the night she died. It gave me the chills. I asked Sergeant Tagliaferro if he thought the killer might be some kind of lunatic, and sending me the jewelry was like gloating over misleading the police. He said he didn't, so I put it out of my mind. Then when I found the poster, it occurred to me that sending it was something else a lunatic might do—you know, warning his victim in advance. I nearly telephoned Sergeant Tagliaferro, only I was afraid of being laughed at. But after last night—" She broke off with a shrug.

"If you're wondering whether I got the same kind of Christmas greeting, I didn't. I can't answer for anything that might have come more recently. I've started chucking out envelopes without return addresses because—Well, I decided it was time to take a stand on junk mail." The lie came out smoothly.

Anita gave me a wan smile. "Strong-minded of you. I could never throw an envelope away without opening it, any more than I could ignore a ringing telephone. I guess I've never lost the childhood expectation that somebody out there might be wanting to offer me the moon."

I slid the pieces of the poster back into the envelope. "Do you mind if I take this? I intend to give it to Sergeant Tagliaferro."

"Better you than me." Anita heaved a sigh of relief. "I've been agonizing all night, wondering if I might be adding two and two and getting five. Maybe the fire was just an accident, but if it wasn't—I don't think you should lose any time getting in touch with the police."

"I couldn't agree more."

"Thank God." Anita came up to me with outstretched arms, embraced me as if she were seeing me off on a round-the-world voyage. "In a way I hoped you'd laugh it off, but in a way I was afraid of that, too. I see I did the right thing, telling you." She let me go and stepped back. "Before you leave, Maggie, there's something I want you to have."

She walked into the closet, stood on tiptoe to reach the back of the overhead shelf, and came down with Paquita, the flamenco doll, resplendent as ever in orchid satin and black lace. "Everything's packed, but if there's something else of Nina's you'd like to have—"

"No, no. This is perfect, absolutely perfect." My eyelids

started to prickle. Paquita had been a legacy from a teacher of flamenco whose arthritic final years Nina had helped ease. "Thank you, Anita."

"I was sure I'd chosen right." Anita's smile was almost blithe as she handed me the doll. But her face became sober again in an instant. "Be careful, Maggie."

I promised I would and left, carrying Paquita like an overgrown baby. In the taxi I studied the manila envelope, trying to recall if I had seen one like it in my mailbox recently. Pointless mental gymnastics. A warning could have been sent in any kind of a wrapper.

Was the poster really a warning? That Anita had been wrong about where the jewelry came from didn't necessarily mean she was wrong about this. She had mentioned adding two and two, and the hackneyed phrase had a hideous resonance. Two and two made four. The number of our group. *Pas de Quatre.* Nina was dead. I'd escaped death by the skin of my teeth.

What about the other two?

I couldn't have come to grips with that one straightaway even if I'd wanted to. I arrived home with barely enough time to set up for my ten o'clock intermediate class, devised for nondancing theater professionals but invariably attended by bona fide ballet dancers, who will take any class going if you let them. Total concentration was required from start to finish, and the same was even more true of the advanced class that followed. I dismissed the burning chariot, the torn poster, all nondance matters from my mind, doing so good a job of it that when Mary Ann Sanders came up to me afterwards and asked if I was going to give class in the afternoon I couldn't for a moment fathom why she should ask. Only for a moment. Then I bristled and said of course, I wasn't a snowflake, and none of my vital parts had melted away. She didn't react to my belligerence, merely turned on her heel and marched out of the studio. I was ashamed of myself, but not enough to call her back and apologize. What was it about the girl that always turned me into a porcupine?

I waited in the studio till I heard no more sounds from the dressing room, checked to make sure everybody was gone, and went down to lock and bolt the front door. The routine I had established after Tagliaferro's warning seemed anything but routine today.

I went up to my apartment and shook the poster pieces out of the manila envelope onto the table. Four of them, exactly the same size—a very deliberate trashing. I fitted them together, feeling as if I were reconstructing a relic of a time almost as remote as the ballet blanc era we had parodied. In the poster we wore costumes derived from the famous *Pas de Quatre* prints of Taglioni and Grisi and Cerrito and Grahn, but instead of forming a graceful cluster we were spread out at the points of the compass, haughtily staring down the camera. I was north, en pointe, arms in third position full of tension, as if I were anchoring an invisible bale of laundry on my head. Nina and Karin Holmquist, east and west, were a matched pair in slightly sickle-footed, flutter-wristed attitudes. Allie Joyce, our Taglioni, was at the peak of a grand battement that was impeccably clean and elegant, yet somehow managed to suggest a can-can. All of us looked incredibly young, incredibly confident.

And each of us had been torn in half, Allie and I vertically, Nina and Karin horizontally. With almost surgical precision. I shuddered and shoved the pieces of the poster back into the envelope.

Suddenly it struck me that if Anita had wanted to spook me, she couldn't have chosen a better way to go about it. Had that been her intention? Was it possible that during all those years of doling out tender loving care and support to Nina and getting hardly anything back she had built up a store of murderous hatred? That killing Nina hadn't exhausted the hatred? That she perceived me as an extension of Nina and—

Sure it was possible. Theoretically, anything was possible. But I didn't believe it for a moment, and formulating wild hypotheses only served to postpone doing what I knew I had to do.

I took my address book off the shelf; turned to the *N*'s; found Karin Nordstrom, née Holmquist. The entry was very old and had never been altered. Karin (with a long *a*—she was very particular about that) was the kind who played it close to the nest, and I sometimes used to wonder how she had ever managed to uproot herself from Minnesota to pursue a ballet career in New York. The transplanting never really took. After the *Pas de Quatre* disbanded, though she could easily have carved out a career on Broadway the way Nina did, she hied herself back home to marry her childhood sweetheart and immediately started dropping babies (four? five? I'd lost count). There was her telephone number right in front of me. All I had to do was pick up the phone and dial. Nothing easier.

Except that I would almost have preferred having a go at thirty-two fouettés, bum leg and all.

I picked up the phone. Dialed. Found myself hoping nobody would pick up at the other end.

Somebody did. "Hello." The soft, measured intonation sounded familiar—and not familiar.

"Karin?"

Silence.

"Hello? I'm trying to reach Karin Holm—Nordstrom. Do I have the right number?"

"You have the right number." The voice had gone flat and toneless. "Who is this anyway?"

"Maggie Tremayne. I used to dance with Karin in New York. May I speak to her please?"

"You can't." Pause. "She's dead."

I went numb all over. The mouthpiece of the phone was in my line of vision, and I marveled how a hand that couldn't feel could still hang on.

"I'm so sorry." Words came—another marvel. "I . . . I didn't know. Are you her daughter?"

"Yes. Kristine. With a *K*."

"I can't tell you how sorry I am, Kristine. How . . . How did it happen?" *Please let it be flu or pneumonia or appendicitis or—*

"She was walking to her Sunday school class when this car—The driver didn't stop. It was an accident, I guess."

Like hell it was. "When?" I winced at the baldness of it. "I mean, only a few months ago I received a Christmas card and—"

"Nine weeks ago." Pause. "If you want to speak to Papa, he's not in."

Papa. Into my mind's eye flashed a silver-framed photograph of a tow-haired youth with a bony face and dark, camera-shy eyes—the first item out of Karin's suitcase in any hotel room.

"Please convey my condolences to him, Kristine. I hope you'll forgive my ringing up like this. It must be very painful, getting a call out of the blue and having to rake up—"

"We're used to it." But I heard a faint choking sound, as if a sob were being swallowed.

I tendered my inadequate apology one more time, exchanged good-byes, and held the receiver to my ear till I heard a click on the line. The hand that couldn't feel somehow reached out and hung up.

It was beginning to look as if somebody had decreed total wipeout for the *Pas de Quatre*. Nina was dead. Karin was dead. I was alive, but not for want of a good try to push me into the next world.

Which left Allie Joyce. The thought of Allie was agonizing at any time, and now—

Thinking wasn't required. Action was. I had to find out if Allie was alive, pure and simple. She had no phone, but I had the number of her landlord in my address book. I turned to it, steeled myself, picked up the phone, dialed. All I got for my effort was a busy signal. A giant downer, and my heart began thumping like a gong. I felt I might explode if I couldn't put uncertainty to rest right away.

A busy signal doesn't necessarily mean a line is busy. Some-times it means two people are dialing the same number at the same time. Or maybe I had dialed the wrong number. I dialed again. Still busy. Well, most of the time a busy signal does mean busy.

I told myself it was only a matter of minutes till I got through. I forced myself to wait out five of them before I dialed again.

Still busy. I decided I couldn't wait any longer, dialed the operator, and told her I needed to cut in, it was an emergency. She told me to hang on and after a silence that seemed endless came back on the line and said she was sorry, the number I requested was out of order. I asked how come the busy signal then and she said she didn't know.

I hung up. Folded my arms into a pillow on the table and put my head down. All of a sudden it felt too heavy to hold up. The floodgates of memory opened wide.

The first time I set eyes on Allie Joyce she walked into Korovskaya's studio as if she owned it. I gawked, and throughout class I couldn't take my eyes off her. Small wonder. She had limbs that went on and on; fabulous extension; turnout close to a hundred and eighty degrees; elevation like an animated illustration of "ballon," up to then a textbook word to me (watching her, I understood what Nijinsky, asked about his famous leap, meant by, "You have just to go up and then pause a little up there"). Everything a dancer longs for, Allie had.

Back then, unfortunately, in the dance world as in the world at large, nobody thought black was particularly beautiful. The day Allie showed up at Korovskaya's, she was fresh from a stint in a German ballet company, where she had danced mostly in tacky revivals of *Scheherazade* and *Cleopatra* and half-baked expressionistic stuff, with an occasional Lilac Fairy or Myrthe thrown in as a sop. She knew only too well that this was better than she could hope for in the States, but she hadn't been able to hack it because of the low level of performance ("a corps of Valkyries, not sylphides—it always sounded like they were wearing wooden shoes"), because she felt she was getting attention for the wrong reasons ("like Topsy, man"), because she was just plain homesick.

I didn't know this or anything else about her at the time. I was just a kid and never got up the nerve to talk to her, which was probably just as well. I might have taken personally her almost bone-chilling aloofness, the attitude that prompted someone to describe her as "an Aida who never lets you forget you should be kneeling to her."

On a stage, Allie was every inch a queen. Korovskaya, whenever the whim struck, used to give recitals for her students, and people would fall all over themselves to donate theaters, costumes, whatever. She gave one during my sophomore year at Barnard. Not the usual medley of variations, pas de deux, and "look-Ma-I'm-dancing" versions of the Garland Waltz—a full-length performance of *The Firebird*. Nowadays the ballet is pretty much a museum piece (remember those performances at NYCB where the denouement looked like a semianimated wedding cake?), and it's hard to get much sense of what Fokine had in mind unless the likes of a Tallchief or a Hayden or a Fonteyn dances the title role and makes sparks fly. Fonteyn wrote in her autobiography that she sought advice on interpretation from Karsavina, who created the role, and was told that the Firebird was "'proud, arrogant . . . powerful, hard to manage, rebellious. . . . Here is no human emotion.'" Korovskaya, a member of the Ballets Russes during the Fokine era, passed on substantially the same message. When Allie came onstage, flashing and flaming in her orange plumage, her legs devouring space, you almost expected to see craters open up where her feet touched down. Her display of fury at being captured by Ivan Tsarevich, a mere mortal, would have made anyone halfway intelligent let go at once, but the plot has Ivan longer on guts than on brains, and he makes the Firebird buy her freedom with a feather and a promise to come to his aid when he needs her. At the point in the ballet when the Firebird keeps her promise and takes on the evil wizard Kostchai, the battle was no contest. I can still rerun Allie's final moments in my mind—the triumphant preparation for takeoff, the leap that traversed half the stage and carried her out of sight.

Korovskaya's recitals were always well attended, and Allie's performance attracted considerable attention. She got a number of offers, but somehow they never came to anything much, perhaps because she was invariably perceived as an ethnic or exotic type and she was a classicist to the core. A few years later, Nina, who attended that memorable *Firebird*, thought of Allie for the Taglioni role in the parody of *Pas de Quatre*. It proved a happier inspiration than anybody expected, for behind that regal black facade was a wild, wicked, absolutely marvelous sense of humor. The handful of years Allie spent clowning with the group provided more sustained creative fulfillment than she had ever known. The night I came down on that accursed floorboard and tore up my knee, everything went smash for her, too.

I didn't know it at the time. Very likely if I had I wouldn't have cared particularly, since I was too deeply immured in Funk City to believe anybody with two good legs could have problems worth bothering about. I didn't see Allie again until Korovskaya's funeral. She looked awful, gaunt and heartbreakingly fragile, with dull, matted hair and a grayish cast to her skin, and she had on immense glasses so dark I wondered how she could see anything. She mentioned that she hadn't been working, and I felt remorseful for having neglected her. I told her I had a studio going and had taken on more than I could handle (a lie—what else did I have to do?), and asked her if she would like to teach classes for me. She went for it, and for a while it worked out just fine. Sharing what she knew seemed to revitalize her; the classes she gave crackled with excitement. Then she seemed to lose interest, showed up late, had somebody phone her in sick, wasn't really there when she was there—the kind of shit you pull when you're trapped in a job you hate. One day she simply didn't turn up. I let off a little steam at my accompanist, who was putting himself through Juilliard primarily by working in cabarets, and he shrugged and said, "What do you expect from a junkie?" It took all my willpower to keep from hitting him over the head with my stick, I wanted so desperately to deny it. I couldn't, though. The skeletal thinness, the diminished attention span, the dark glasses—it all added up.

Back then, to keep from playing ostrich, I'd had to vanquish a shabby little demon telling me in the voice of reason that Allie's problem was none of my business, there was nothing I could do.

Old adversaries never seem to die. I felt now that I would give just about anything for a nice sandbox.

I was the only white person on the bus.

Nine years ago, when I made up my mind I wasn't going to turn my back on Allie and went up to Harlem to see her, I was the only white person on the bus. I was very nervous. It was around Thanksgiving, I remember, and I sat in back next to a window with a decal of a turkey on it and studied a street map the whole way, raising my head only to look at street signs, avoiding eye contact with other passengers. I got off the bus on legs stiff as stilts. Strangely, negotiating the streets wasn't as bad as I expected. Oh, I drew any number of stares, none friendly, and a few people looked past me as if I weren't there, but I didn't feel that unsafe. Maybe because what I saw looked so much like the nongentrified parts of my own neighborhood. Overflowing garbage cans and graffiti are the same everywhere.

I found Allie's street without difficulty, thanks to the map. Her building had a faded red-brick facade with the number still in place on the lintel of the outside door, though the door itself was missing. In the vestibule, only a few of the mailboxes had names in the slots and fewer still had functioning locks. There was an inner door with no lock at all, just a hole under the doorknob. The hall smelled of stale food and urine and animals, with a faint tang of pesticide. The worn blue linoleum on the floor wasn't clean, but it wasn't filthy either. The stairs were solid, with wide treads that obviously saw a broom now and again. At the top of the first flight, the building smell began to give way to the smell of baking apples heavily laced with cinnamon; it got stronger as I went up to the next flight to the third floor, Allie's floor. I quickened my pace, feeling better about things. Where somebody was baking, all couldn't be wrong with the world.

The smell was coming from the door at the top of the stairs. At a logical guess, 3A, and the next door over would be 3B, Allie's apartment. But building layouts frequently have nothing to do with logic, and there were no numbers on any of the doors on the landing. The prospect of knocking on the wrong door was daunting. I plumped for the cinnamon and apples, lifted the brass knocker shaped like a lamb's head and let it fall. The reverberation was loud and a long time fading away.

The door opened partway, shadowing the room inside. The woman in the doorway was tall and slim, with a regal carriage, and for an instant I thought she was Allie. She stepped forward into the light of the hall, and I saw that her face was a patchwork of brown and russet and tan and cream, like the hide of a piebald pony. She stared at me with great dark eyes—Allie's eyes. I asked for Allie and she said Allie wasn't home, in a slightly raspy voice I recognized from telephone conversations. I told her who I was and said I'd come to see if Allie was all right, if there was anything I could do, playing it dumb because how else was there to play it? She continued to stare at me for a moment, then said, flatly, "Go home," and stepped back inside.

But I wasn't about to leave it at that. I cast about for something, anything, to keep that door from shutting in my face, and I blurted that I had some good news for Allie. The marred face was in darkness, but I didn't have to see it to read it. What could be good news for Allie?

"She has some money coming to her."

I'd said the magic word. The door opened wide and I walked into a big, square room dominated by a massive steaming black oven and several rows of baker's racks, most of them filled with pies. The cinnamon-laden warmth seemed to embrace me, and I felt cozy and safe, as if I'd stepped back into the womb.

The dark eyes that were so much like Allie's questioned me, and I explained that the money involved was the long-delayed settlement from a lawsuit filed years ago against a theatrical agent who had bilked the *Pas de Quatre* of the proceeds from a tour. To my ears it sounded like the crock it was, but she didn't ask any questions, not even how much was involved. Her eyes grew luminous with joy, and she said, "Praise the Lord. You keep it for her. Send a check to landlord every month long as it last, else it won't do her a particle of good. Hang on." She glided out of the room; returned in a moment with a piece of paper and thrust it into my hand and closed my fingers over it. "Landlord's address. Now I know she stay put so's I can watch over her. Praise the Lord."

The next thing I knew I was back out in the hall and the door was closing in my face. I started toward the stairs, but something made me change course and walk over to the next door and put my ear against it. Inside, someone was humming softly, dreamily—the waltz from Act One of *Giselle*. I raced down the stairs with scalding eyes.

I made no further attempts to get in touch with Allie, just sent the checks to her landlord every month. Acknowledgment came in the form of periodic requests for increases, not extortionate as these things go. Allie was staying put. That she was also "well" and "comfortable" I knew from handwritten postscripts to Christmas cards bearing printed assurances that the Lord was watching over me, one way or another (last Christmas He had been holding me close to His heart).

I had no map with me on the bus this time, nothing to shield me from inimical stares, but I was beyond worrying about them, overt hostility that I could account for seeming tame compared with what I had to worry about closer to home. It was still light when I got out, and I found I remembered the way. Debris in front of Allie's building—a kite with a long, jagged rent, a roller skate minus a wheel, a baby carriage filled with empty whiskey bottles. There was an outer door now, an unpainted steel affair that looked as if it had been lifted from a bunker or a prison. The inner door still lacked a lock. Inside, the odor of disinfectant was so strong my eyes started to tear, and I ran up the stairs hoping to get away from it. No warm, cinnamon-rich aroma offered the illusion of sanctuary today, not even when I came right up to the door at the top of the third-floor landing.

The response to my knock was prompt, almost as if I were expected, and the door opened wide. The woman's face was the vivid, almost garish mélange of color I remembered, only it looked half a century older. I could guess why. My heart plummeted.

But I hadn't come to guess. I had to *know*.

I wanted to ask, I had to ask—and I couldn't ask. Confronting the disfigured, anguished face was momentarily too much for me, and I had to look away. No steam was coming out of the big black oven. The baker's racks were empty. But my nostrils picked up a faint whiff of cinnamon. Baking had been done fairly recently. Life was going on.

I forced myself to look at the woman's face again, rigidly composed, like a wood carving. She wasn't about to give me any help. Well, why should she give me any help?

"Tell me how—about Allie."

"Nothin' to tell." Her face contorted for an instant. "Fell out the window."

It wasn't unexpected. I wasn't unprepared. And still I had to walk across the room and grab hold of a rack to make sure of staying on my feet.

"I can't tell you how sorry I am. When . . . When did it happen?"

"Seven weeks ago. Fifty-one days."

And how many hours? Minutes? Seconds? I didn't doubt she knew. "I can't tell you how sorry I am." It sounded even lamer the second time.

She shrugged. "Been gone a whole lot longer than that. Didn't see no purpose to no big service. Reckon I should have let you know sooner'n I did, but figured long as I wrote you before the rent come due—"

"No problem." I had paid the rent as usual; no doubt her letter was among those I had discarded unopened. "The reason I came—Is there anything I can do for you? Anything you need?"

The spectre of a smile twitched the corners of her mouth. "Like some more money somebody owed Allie? She got a big laugh out of that one. No, I don't need nothin' from you. You already done more than you should. Wouldn't have let you only I didn't have no choice. Wanted her to move in with me, but she wouldn't. Keepin' her next door was next best. At least I knew where she was at. I appreciate that."

"It was little enough. I wish I could have done more. Are you sure there isn't anything I can do for you now?"

"Don't need nothin'." Once again, the patchwork face turned to wood. "You can tell the other lady the same, so's she won't be comin' 'round."

"The other lady?" I echoed stupidly. But deep down I knew what was coming. Fortunately, I was still holding on to the rack.

"From the group. Little bitty redhead. Didn't leave no address, so I couldn't write her. She come up here to help, same as you. Say she try and get Allie into a program, but Allie just look at her and say 'Why?' So redhead say okay, she gonna see to it Allie get what she need. I don't like it, I know it ain't right. But if it keep her happy—" Tears began to course down the mottled cheeks. "Dougie come round regular, say that for him. She didn't have to do any of the bad stuff. Thought she was okay. Didn't know how blue she get sometimes. Didn't know one day she get so blue she just open up the window and step out into her grave."

"But she didn't," I blurted, and could have kicked myself. "I mean, it could very well have been an accident. When people trip out they often think they can fly." How plausible it sounded.

If only it were true.

"No way. She just up and go." The tears continued to flow, in big, pear-shaped drops. "From the time she a little girl she talk a lot about havin' wings nobody could see. Her way of shuttin' people out. Time was she shut me out cause she be shamed of me in front of her downtown friends. Then she start shuttin' out the downtown friends, shuttin' out everybody. Say she goin' to a place where she keep her wings forever and ever, nobody can take them away from her. Make no sense to me."

It did to me. The sylphide, by throwing in her lot with a mortal, loses her wings and dies. Allie had chosen to soar where nobody could follow her, touch her, talk to her—the ultimate cop-out. Or maybe choice wasn't in it. I thought of Vaslav Nijinsky and Olga Spessivtzeva, transported to God knows where and sealed off from pursuit by madness.

All these years Nina had been helping Allie take flight. It wouldn't have been difficult for her to arrange those regular drug deliveries, not with a Larry Sondergaard in her past. But it didn't have to be Sondergaard. If you can believe what you hear, doctors and lawyers and stockbrokers and other ostensible paragons of respectability are big entrepreneurs in the drug trade these days. Still, however Nina had arranged it, she must have put herself to some degree of risk with absolutely nothing to gain, not even thanks. I wished with all my heart she had confided in me. But why should she have? Telling anybody would only have increased the risk.

"Never did let redhead know I appreciate what she try to do. Been on my conscience. If it ain't too much trouble, maybe you could do it for me."

"I can't—" I checked myself and forced a smile; I was afraid the skin of my face would crack over the bones. "I can't believe she would want you to fret about thanking her. She wanted to help Allie, that's all. Just as I did."

"You done what you could and I thank you for it, but I wish she'd never heard of dancin'. Her second-grade teacher got her started—had a sister worked for Katherine Dunham. Pretty soon she wantin' to study downtown. First I say no, don't want her gettin' big ideas sure to go up in smoke. Next thing I know, that old Russian teacher look like a witch come to see me, tell me I can't stand in Allie's way. So I had to let her go, and sure enough it lead to one disappointment after another. Then you people come along and give her a chance to work regular and make her real happy. She always say bein' in the group the best thing ever happen to her."

"It was a privilege to share a stage with her. She was the one doing us a favor. I know the others would say the same if—if they were here."

I nearly choked on the last part. Spokesperson for the dead isn't the most comfortable of roles, especially if you've barely escaped joining their number and have reason to fear you might not escape next time.

For there was sure to be a next time. Somebody had indeed decreed total wipeout for the *Pas de Quatre*. Somehow or other, we had managed to inspire lethal enmity while we were working our tails off to make people laugh, while Allie was having the best time of her life, while I was having the best time of mine, while Nina and Karin were having, if not the best times of their lives, damn good times.

Who wanted us all dead? Why? Above all, why now, two decades after the breakup of the group?

As if to shove me deeper into Necropolis, a photograph of the four of us, relaxing in practice clothes, was held up in front of my face.

"—all I got. The rest was hangin' up on the wall next door, so many you could hardly see the paint. When she . . . went, they was all gone. Burned them, I reckon."

Not Allie. Not in a million years. "I have plenty of pictures. I'll be happy to send you some."

A glimmer of animation on the wooden carving. "Sure would appreciate havin' something to hold on to. I birthed her and I buried her and a lot of what come in between is kind of a blur.

Don't mind losin' the bad stuff but seems a pity to lose the good."

I promised to send her the pictures straightaway. She said, "Praise the Lord," and held out a hand shaped like Allie's, dark like Allie's. I said again how sorry I was, and then, just as I had nine years before, I fled.

Chapter 12

I n the morning glad I see
My foe outstretch'd beneath the tree.

I couldn't get Blake's verses out of my head; they rattled around through an interminable night. The tree in question is sowed by pent-up anger, nurtured by more of the same until it bears a poisoned apple that destroys the object of that anger. Not really applicable, I kept telling myself. Poetry can overleap a lot of intermediate stages to get from cause to effect.

But the annals of psychiatry are crammed with instances of overleaping those intermediate stages.

When Sergeant Tagliaferro suggested that the motive for Nina's murder might lie in the past, I had pooh-poohed the idea. It still seemed fantastic that anybody could have held a grudge against the entire *Pas de Quatre* all these years. But obviously somebody had, unless a rapid sequence of hit-and-run death, apparent suicide, murder, and near-incineration among four people who had gone separate ways since the group disbanded was merely coincidence. If you could believe that, you were a potential customer for any bridge in the city.

Who? Why? Why *now*?

Practically the minute I got home from Harlem I had extricated my collection of *Pas de Quatre* photographs from the lower depths of the storage room and forced myself to look through them carefully, hoping to jog my memory. The group had started out by spoofing the past and outmoded styles and, inevitably, branched out to include living legends. Choreographers in particular—we took off Balanchine, Frederick Ashton, Antony Tudor, Jerome Robbins, Agnes de Mille, Roland Petit, and pretty much everybody who was anybody at the time. Had we offended people? No doubt we had. You can't do parody without offending somebody. But goading somebody to murder? The closest thing to a complaint we ever had was a report that Tudor had said "We are not amused" to our *Phallus of Flame*, which reached us third hand (as did a report that Nora Kaye *had* been amused). Parody is no rarer in the dance world than in any other, and birds at the top of the tree expect to have their feathers ruffled now and then.

But suppose for the sake of argument we had come down too hard on somebody's toes. Besides the targeted dancers and choreographers, there were balletomanes who might have taken umbrage. And why draw the line at those our performances might have offended? The *Pas de Quatre* had come in contact with impresarios, agents, musicians, stagehands, not to mention personnel of hotels, restaurants, airlines. They all had toes.

Contemplating the pictures proved fruitless, but I hadn't really expected anything else. If we had ever trodden hard enough to break any bones, I would remember. Surely I wouldn't have forgotten an occasion that could have infuriated anybody to the point of wanting all four of us laid out on slabs.

Unless it was something I had never known about. Maybe

somebody in the group had inflicted an insufferable wound or committed an unforgivable sin and the long-postponed vengeance had reached out to encompass us all. Which of us? Inconceivable that it could have been Karin. Allie? Maybe some fanatical racist had taken exception to that imperious aloofness of hers or to the idea of an integrated ballet group and brooded over it for two decades. It sounded unlikely, but what didn't? Back to where it had all seemed to start—Nina, with her rackety social life and her propensity for riding roughshod over whatever got in her way. But even Sergeant Tagliaferro had been underwhelmed by the down-the-road murder potential of a bitchery that had always been up front and aroused the kind of antagonism that was pretty much up front, too.

> I was angry with my foe:
> I told it not, my wrath did grow.
>
> And I water'd it in fears,
> Night and morning with my tears;
> And I sunned it with smiles,
> And with soft deceitful wiles.

I kept coming back to "A Poison Tree."

What else was there to come back to? It had to be a crazy. Had to.

But what if it wasn't? What if there was a rational explanation that my mind was blotting out?

Round and round and round| and | round. |All| cy|linders going. All night long.

I was a wreck in the morning. I went through my first class on semiautomatic pilot, and sympathetic glances from my theater professionals assured me that they understood and forgave. That should have been mortifying. Under normal circumstances, I pride myself on never allowing anything to interfere with my classroom concentration. But what was normal? I could hardly remember.

For my second class, I managed to get myself up to the mark. I'm a professional, too, after all. The thought that the hour when I would be able to dish off yesterday's discoveries to Sergeant Tagliaferro was drawing closer helped considerably.

Everybody's professionalism broke down together. "In a moment, in the twinkling of an eye," as the baritone in *The Messiah* sings just before that trumpet sounds.

It happened while my students were performing grand adagio to Debussy's *La plus que lente*, soft and dreamy music providing no cover for any sounds of intrusion, but nobody heard a thing. All at once the music stopped and Mary Ann Sanders rose straight up from the piano bench with a bug-eyed stare.

In the doorway was a giant wreath of lilies with a white satin banner inscribed IN MEMORIAM MARGARET TREMAYNE in black letters. That's all I saw at first. That's probably all anybody saw at first.

The wreath started moving. Not by itself, though for a wild moment I thought it might be attached to the legs in the baggy charcoal trousers and shiny black loafers that squeaked on the wooden floor. Then I spotted an eye peering out of the lilies.

Astonishingly, I wasn't rooted to the spot. I walked toward the wreath, my soft slippers squeaking a little, too. Snatched it up and flung it to the floor. Found myself confronting a skinny black fourteen year old with wide eyes and gaping jaw and Adam's apple bobbing a mile a minute.

"Who sent this?"

The boy gulped a few times, but no words came out.

"Now look, I'm Maggie Tremayne and I'm still alive and kicking. *Who sent this?*"

The boy closed his mouth. With a quaking finger, he pointed to an engraved pewter button on his lapel: "Stanley's Floral Arrangements." He started backing away from me.

"Wait! Take that monstrosity with you!"

He turned and ran, clattering down the stairs. Fleeing a ghost.

That was the end of class. I didn't dismiss anybody. I didn't have to. My students melted silently away. When they were gone, so was the wreath, and I felt a surge of gratitude for the display of tact. Part of me hoped they would make the wreath disappear altogether, but I knew it had to remain for Tagliaferro to see. I started out of the studio.

Mary Ann blocked my way, all schoolmarmy self-possession again. "Do you intend to cancel your afternoon classes?" Her eyes, regarding me without warmth or expression, made me think of the pale blue marbles that were so highly prized when I was a kid.

I had a sudden, totally irrational impulse to slide my hands under the collar of that neat white shirt and throttle her. Because she had lost her cool? Because she had recovered it? Because she was handy?

"Over some sickie's idea of a joke? Not likely."

"I'll see you later then." She turned and walked out of the studio. Her shoes went clackety-clack-clack down the stairs. The front door opened, closed with a snap.

I went out of the studio and into the dressing room. A sudden, absolute silence greeted me.

"Would you leave the wreath, please? I want it for a souvenir."

I returned to the studio to wait until everybody was gone so I could lock up downstairs for the midday hiatus. My new design for living. Literally.

Rita Ames, a redheaded actress with a spring like a Mexican jumping bean, came back into the studio, dazzling in oversize blue and green and purple striped cowl-neck sweater, purple ski pants, knee-high green suede boots. "If you're into getting even and want a helping hand, just ask. That's from all of us."

"Thanks, Rita. I'll keep it in mind."

"À bientôt!" She blew me a kiss and bounced out of the studio and down the stairs, on her way to give a few tourists a thrill.

I waited in the studio until the building was silent and went to check out the dressing room. Everybody was gone. Only the wreath remained, propped against the wall. I went up to the loathsome thing and tipped it forward. On the back was a card. I tore it off and tucked it into the waistband of my skirt and went downstairs to lock up. I took a good hard look at the niche behind the stairs before I started back up.

The phone began ringing as I reached the studio landing, and I ran up the second flight to answer it. My "Hello" was probably a bit breathless, but nothing to warrant the gasp at the other end.

"Hello?"

"Oh my God. Oh my God." Thea Davidson's unmistakable whisper. "Who is this?"

"Who would it be, Thea?"

"Maggie? Is it really you? Thank God! I thought—Well, what else was there to think? When one receives a formal notification of someone's demise—"

"You received *what?*"

"An engraved black-bordered announcement of your death. In the mail. It looked absolutely genuine. Really, Maggie, if this is some kind of practical joke—"

"Not of mine, Thea. Tell me everything you can about the thing."

For all practical purposes she already had, the only additional information being that the envelope was postmarked Manhattan. She would have liked nothing better than to speculate on whys and wherefores, but I wanted no part of that, said I had tons to do, and disengaged. I knew she would be back on the phone the minute she hung up on me, spreading the news far and wide that reports of my death were greatly exaggerated. The farther and wider the better. I was willing to bet that engraved, black-bordered announcements had gone out to practically everybody I knew.

The phone went again the instant I hung up. I waited for the ringing to stop so I could telephone Stanley's Floral Arrangements. It went on for quite some time, long enough for me to reorder my priorities. When I picked up the receiver, the number I dialed wasn't Stanley's.

"Hello." My mother's voice sounded cautious, almost timorous.

"Hello, Mother. It's me."

"And about time, too." Irascible now—that was more like it. "I've been trying to reach you for hours. Ever since—The phone kept ringing and ringing. Where were you?"

"Teaching class. Just like any other morning." I hesitated. "You got one of those things in the mail, I suppose."

"Indeed we did. Your father was very upset. I took it for black humor. Something I've never acquired a taste for."

"I know, Mother."

"Naturally, I knew it had to be bogus because of the 'Margaret,' so I wasn't alarmed. I was *angry*."

"I know, Mother. I'm pretty angry myself."

"Well, I should hope so. You *are* my daughter."

I had to smile in spite of myself. The acknowledgment had been a rarity for much of my adult life. My mother might have named me after Maggie Teyte (the diminutive was on my birth certificate; she hadn't wanted to run the risk of "Meg" or "Peggy") and got me hooked on ballet, but she never accepted my becoming a dancer, any better than she would have accepted my joining the Roller Derby or a tag team of mud wrestlers. I've always suspected that she viewed my injury and the breakup of my marriage as consequences of going off the rails. My decision to open the studio, in the teeth of her repeated reminders that it was never too late for graduate school, must have disappointed her all over again, though to do her justice she never said so.

"Maggie—" The timorous note was back in my mother's voice. "When I opened the envelope . . . Well, they sometimes get things wrong, you know."

"I know, Mother."

"I thought the most likely possibility was that someone had seized on the terrible thing that happened to Nina to play a nasty joke on you, but of course sometimes lightning does strike twice and—" A long pause. "It *is* just a joke, isn't it? There really isn't anything wrong?"

"No, Mother. Everything's fine. Don't worry."

"All right." Another pause, and then, softly, "Thank you for calling."

I hung up with guilt pangs gnawing at me: some things never change. The phone started ringing immediately. Twelve rings, and it stopped. A superstitious caller? I've been told that the dial tone doesn't actually correspond to the ringing at the other end, but I don't know whether that's true.

I dialed the number on the card I'd taken off the wreath. Two buzzes, and the receiver at the other end was picked up. "Stanley's Floral Arrangements. Stanley here. Good day to you." The voice was a nasal singsong, slightly bored.

"I'd like to find out who ordered the wreath that was delivered to my studio a little while ago. Inscribed 'In Memoriam Margaret Tremayne.'"

"Oh yes." No longer bored. Wary. Undoubtedly he'd had the delivery boy's report. "I'm afraid I can't tell you that."

"Privileged information?" My tone might have made the sturdiest cabbage leaf curl up and shrivel.

"Nothing like that, Ms. Tremayne. I can't tell you because I don't know. The order came in the mail with a cash enclosure. I have it right here. Typewritten. No signature or return address."

"Didn't that strike you as peculiar?"

"Not really. People often send flowers anonymously. It's rather an easy way to assuage guilt feelings, don't you know. But I assure you that in my twenty-three years in the business nothing like *this* has ever happened before. I'm genuinely sorry to have caused you such distress, however unwittingly. Is there any way I can make amends?"

It was on the tip of my tongue to suggest he might send another wreath addressed to Lady Lazarus. I thanked him with as much civility as I could muster and asked him to hang on to the typewritten order for the police, realizing, as I said it, that the police would undoubtedly want to see the black-bordered announcement as well and that I should have asked Thea to hang on to hers. Stanley assured me he would "hang on for dear life" and expressed his regrets again.

I thought about ringing Thea back, decided not to. Her line would be busy, and anyway there would be plenty of other announcements floating around. Chances were they would lead nowhere because the order to the printer had been anonymous, too.

I reminded myself that all this was the concern of professionals, not me. Tagliaferro was due back this afternoon, so I didn't have much longer before I could dump it all on him. That should have provided comfort, but somehow it didn't.

The telephone started ringing again. I didn't pick up. It went on ringing and ringing and ringing. Some paragon of persistence? Or was there a seamless join where one caller hung up and another took over?

As if it mattered. Since when had I developed such a burning interest in the inner workings of Ma Bell et al.?

The ringing stopped.

I felt bereft. As if my lifeline had been wrenched away. Idiotic. Or was it? What if Tagliaferro had checked in early, heard about an unnamed woman trying to reach him, connected the woman with me, tried to return my call? That could explain the marathon ringing, couldn't it?

I dialed the police. Tagliaferro wasn't back yet, of course. This time I left my name and a message for him to call me, saying it was urgent. I was asked if somebody else would do. I mulled it over for a moment, reminded myself that I was safe in my little cocoon until Tagliaferro called or my four o'clock class arrived, and said no thanks.

Hanging up, I felt the lifeline go once again. It occurred to me that the cocoon analogy was a bit scary: if the world at large was sealed out, the pupa was just as effectively sealed in.

Nobody out there could touch me, that was the thing to hold on to. *Nobody out there could touch me.* The words became a litany, and I ran them through my mind over and over again, a silent tape.

The tape stopped running. Suddenly. As if the power button had been pushed.

I had heard a noise. A faint thump, like something falling. It came from directly below, where there shouldn't be a sound. One thing I could be certain of—nothing human had caused it. I had made sure everybody was out of the building before I locked the front door.

Had I? What if somebody had been hiding in the niche under the stairs, sneaked up here to my apartment while I was in the studio or the dressing room, and sneaked down to the studio while I was locking up?

Pretty farfetched. It would presuppose somebody who was familiar with every inch of the building, creaking stair tread and all. Somebody who knew my habits inside out.

But wasn't it obvious by now that was precisely the sort of somebody I was dealing with?

My heart was thumping away like crazy, and I had difficulty catching my breath. I told myself that I might have been mistaken about the source of the noise, that it might have come from the street. Always supposing I hadn't imagined a noise in the first place.

I listened. I felt as if every pore in my body were wide open, I was listening so hard. Not a sound except my pounding heart and my ragged breathing. Then, far away, a motorcycle revved up. A horn honked. Silence again.

If I heard a noise inside the building, chances were a mouse had made it. Mice were no strangers here. One of Milton Frankovich's patients had fainted when a mouse scampered across his consulting room floor, and I had a vivid memory of a sighting in the dressing room and the ensuing hysterics.

Tomorrow I would call the exterminator. A fine resolution,

based as it was on the assumption that there would be a tomorrow.

My heartbeat quieted. My breathing eased. Willpower. What I had to do next was get myself moving. Down those stairs to check out the studio and the dressing room and prove to myself everything was as it should be. A tall order.

I looked around my living space, gilded by the sunlight pouring through the windows. Now there was something to take real comfort in. Spooks don't operate in broad daylight.

God, I was in bad shape, seeking comfort in the idea of a mouse and in the reputed habits of spooks.

I got to my feet and walked to the door. Easy. Nothing to it.

I put on the brakes. If there was anything to the notion that an intruder had sneaked in and holed up, then I had to search the entire building, so might as well start up here.

I made an about face and searched thoroughly. The loft first, where nobody was under the bed. Neither was anybody in the john or in the storage room or in any of the closets or crouched behind a chair or scrunched up in a cupboard. Not that I expected there would be. What kept me from feeling like a complete idiot was remembering the night I hadn't expected to find anybody in the building and found Bridget Foster.

Well, it wouldn't be Bridget this time.

Most likely it wouldn't be anybody.

I went out to the hall, stopped at the top of the stairs, again listening intently, again hearing nothing. I was sorely tempted to call out "Who's there?" Absurd, any way you looked at it. Either I would be talking to myself or to somebody who had a vested interest in not responding.

I started down the stairs. Not on tiptoe. With my normal step. I didn't avoid the creaking tread. I had every right to walk down these stairs. It was the trespasser who should be worrying.

Common sense said there wasn't any trespasser.

I stopped at the bottom of the stairs. Suddenly frozen. Suddenly fearful of setting foot in my own studio. If a million cacodemons had put their heads together to dream up the ultimate punishment for all my sins, this would be it.

Fear gave way to anger. The studio was my turf. *Mine.* Nobody was going to take it away from me.

I forced myself to start moving again. Stepped over the studio threshold. Stopped in my tracks.

Propped up against the piano, facing me, was the wreath of lilies with the white satin banner screaming IN MEMORIAM MARGARET TREMAYNE. The wreath I had last seen in the dressing room when I removed Stanley's card from the back. No chance my mind was playing tricks this time.

Now that I had a legitimate reason to be frightened, I wasn't. I felt calm. Resigned to my fate. Whatever this was all about, I was going to find out at last. I walked up to the wreath and touched it. Definitely not an illusion. Somebody had carried it out of the dressing room and in here.

Still I didn't feel frightened. The calmness that had hold of me was uncanny. I had sense enough—just—to realize it was a bad thing.

Sluggishly, my instinct for self-preservation came alive, counseled flight. But even if I'd had the right reaction instantaneously, it wouldn't have made a bit of difference. When I turned to run, Mary Ann Sanders stood in the doorway with a gun in her hand. The gun was pointed at me and it looked enormous.

"Surprise, surprise," said Mary Ann. An almost unrecognizable Mary Ann, in spite of the prim knot of hair and the rimless glasses, the serviceable and unstylish getup that had become a familiar feature of my studio scene over the past months. On her face was a look I had never seen there before. Radiant. Exultant. With anybody else, I would have assumed it was the glow of lovemaking, anticipated or fulfilled.

A stirring at the back of my mind. I recalled Stu Cottman at the party the night Nina was killed, pawing Mary Ann and telling her he knew she was ready for it, he had seen the look on her face. At the time I had put it down to drunken befuddlement.

I felt the blood congealing in my veins. I couldn't take my eyes from the gun.

"I know how to use it, in case you're wondering." Mary Ann's tone was as matter-of-fact as usual.

"I wasn't." I knew what her hands could do on the keyboard of a piano. How could I doubt their proficiency at anything they turned to?

She came into the studio, the Mary Ann I knew and a total stranger. I started to back away, but the gun jerked and I came forward. As if body and soul were in thrall to the menacing black metal, I had to stop, go, shake a limb on command—like Petrouchka.

I should have been scared out of my wits. God knows I had sufficient cause, and no doubt deep down inside of me the terror was bottled up, waiting to erupt. But that curious calmness still had hold of me. My head felt oddly light, ready to detach and float away and leave my body to fend for itself.

"Why?" I asked. More to get my mind involved than for any other reason. As soon as the question was out, though, I wanted to know the answer in the worst way. "*Why*, Mary Ann?"

The exultation left her face; it became stern and self-righteous, the face of the teacher giving you those ten hours of detention you deserve a hundred times over. "Because of what you did to Mother, of course."

That got my mind involved all right. It started working furiously, but to no purpose. How could I have done anything to someone I didn't know? I had never heard of Mary Ann until the day last summer when she walked into the studio to ask for a job, and all I'd ever seen of her mother was the photograph on the piano in her apartment. What could I remember about that photograph? Not very much. Skinned-back pale hair, flesh pinched over the bones, wide, myopic-looking blue eyes— features that made me recognize her at once as Mary Ann's mother, but there had been no other recognition involved.

How could I have done anything to someone I didn't know?

Maybe it wasn't me, specifically, who had done whatever had been done to Mary Ann's mother. Maybe another member of the *Pas de Quatre* had known her and—

"You haven't the slightest idea what I'm talking about, have you?"

"Quite honestly, no."

"That's rich. That's really rich." She smiled more widely than I had ever seen her smile, baring her teeth to the gumline. "You really don't remember a thing about it."

So much for the idea that it was somebody else, not me. There was, obviously, something for me to remember. But what? My mind was still racing, still getting nowhere. I looked at those strong-looking teeth, the color of old ivory, the color of the keys of the Steinway. I looked at the pale blue eyes, glittering behind the glasses. Mary Ann's face was an animated version of the photograph, therefore should have provided a clue. It didn't.

"When I was a little girl and Mother used to tell me what you did, I used to wonder how you managed it. Did he spend a night with each of you in turn? Did he make the rounds every night? Did you all collect in one room and have orgies? All of the above?"

A glimmer at the back of my mind, like a light at the end of a long, long tunnel.

"It didn't faze any of you one little bit, thrusting yourselves between a man and his lawful wife, trampling on a bond sanctified before God. And naturally it didn't mean a thing to you that you broke my mother's heart. You don't even remember it."

The glimmer was full illumination now. I remembered all right. Remembered how all four of us had joined in a charade as a favor to our musical arranger. Horror welled up inside me as I realized how powerless I was before the consequences of the deception propagated all those years ago.

Three lifetimes ago. About to be four.

"I suppose it isn't surprising you can't keep track. The name you've forgotten is Terence Sablier."

"I haven't forgotten it." Why hadn't I made the connection between Terry and Mary Ann sooner? "Sablier" meant "Sandman"—only a quarter step removed from "Sanders." Though Mary Ann didn't look much like Terry, the musicality they shared should have been some kind of giveaway.

What if I had made the connection? A clairvoyant might have had trouble seeing this coming.

"You must have a remarkable memory. Or do you notch the bedpost?"

I had all I could do to keep from flinching. During those lost, I-don't-give-a-damn years after my accident, I had bedded down pretty indiscriminately. From a certain point of view, that made a bond with the others. Nina, of course, had been promiscuous all her life. Karin had succumbed briefly to the blandishments of a sugar daddy, and for Allie chastity had never held the highest priority. From a certain point of view, the four of us might well appear a quartet of man-eaters.

Man-eaters. I suddenly recalled a night in Cleveland when we danced our parody of Robbins's *The Cage*, in which, instead of frenzied, mate-devouring insects gyrating to Stravinsky, we were laid-back cats stretching to Satie; at the end the Tom (me) was popped into a giant oven and, in anticipation of microwaves, roasted in an instant with a flickering red spotlight. After the performance, a marching band of radical feminists came backstage to congratulate us on the efforts we were making for the cause. We knew better than to issue any disclaimers. Anybody who has ever set foot on a stage knows that what an audience derives from a performance often hasn't much to do with what's put into it. People see what they want to see, what they're conditioned to see.

When performers concentrate on sending a message and the audience is primed to receive it, the impact has to be a blockbuster.

Long, long ago the *Pas de Quatre* had acted up a storm to create an image of Terry Sablier as a womanizer. A harmless performance for an audience of one, we had thought, and forgotten about it practically the minute it was over.

Harmless. Three of us were dead, and if Mary Ann had her way, I would complete the tally.

There had to be a way to stop it. Had to. "You're making a terrible mistake," I babbled. "It wasn't the way you think it was." Even to my own ears it sounded like the lamest of back-to-the-wall excuses.

The knuckles on the hand gripping the gun turned white. "Wasn't it? Are you going to deny that you pulled out all the stops to get my father to work for your wretched little group? Thanks to you he forgot he had a wife, forgot he had a child. If there's been any mistake, *you* made it."

I opened my lips, closed them again. What could I say? "You've got it all wrong, Mary Ann. Your father wasn't a Don Juan, he was gay and afraid to come out of the closet. Want proof? Go outside and walk a few blocks down Columbus Avenue to Donnie Buell's pad and you'll find a shrine dedicated to Terence Sablier, the great love of Donnie's life." The truth, but no chance in the world she would believe it. Not when the lie we had acted out so long ago had ossified into holy writ. Very likely she would blow me away where I stood.

"You aren't denying it, I see. Because you can't. Because you must have known in your heart of hearts that what you were doing was wrong, evil, a sin before God. But you didn't care, did you? Maybe you even laughed about how easily you got him away from Mother. You know what he told her? He told her to go back home to Oak Grove and wipe him out of her mind and find somebody else. After all they'd been to each other. Can you believe it?"

I could. Sensible advice, under the circumstances. Also the kind of advice that nobody ever listens to.

"I know what you're thinking. I can read you like a book by

now, Maggie Tremayne. You're thinking that's what she should have done, aren't you?"

"More or less. She was still young. She was still—" I swallowed hard. "She still had her looks. However badly she'd been hurt, she had her whole life ahead of her." The banality reverberated in the void as I remembered myself, freshly afflicted with the same kind of hurt. If Junior had handed me the "forget-me-and-find-somebody-else" line, I would probably have bashed him over the head with my cane.

What if Junior had died after walking out on me? Would I have stopped resenting him? I couldn't summon up an unqualified affirmative, God help me.

"Her whole life," Mary Ann echoed, a tight little smile tugging up the corners of her mouth. "What kind of a life? After he died, Mother did go back to Oak Grove. And you know what? Everybody knew the marriage had broken up. *His* family had spread their version of things around, I guess. Anyhow, Mother wasn't able to hold her head up. How could she prove the failure wasn't hers? If a man turns away from his wife, people believe it's at least partly her fault. Mother could tell what people thought from the way they looked at her. Even the children looked at her like that—she had to stop giving piano lessons. It was awful for her. It killed her, as sure as we're standing here. *You* killed her."

Protest rose to my lips. I didn't voice it.

The smile that wasn't really a smile got bigger. "At least you're not saying you don't know what I'm talking about anymore. That's progress, I guess. I'm sure you think I'm exaggerating, but I'm not. Mother was sensitive. She minded what people thought about her. Little by little she shut herself away from the world because there was nothing left in it for her. Do you know what it's like to watch somebody wither away? I grew up doing it. Ever since I can remember I've known why. Ever since I can remember I've known who the enemy was. Ever since—You were going to say something?"

"Nothing of any consequence. Just that it seems like a terrible burden to place on a child."

"You're right, it isn't of any consequence. I was proud to share Mother's burdens. When I was a baby, she used to wish I'd never been born. But when I started to be a real person, she changed her mind. I don't know how many times she told me I was the best thing in her life. We were so close. We shared everything. She taught me to play the piano because she loved music so much and wanted me to love it, too. She said one day I would be a better musician than *he* was. I had to work so hard to please her, sometimes I thought I'd drop at the piano, but I didn't really mind. I loved her so much, I would have done anything for her. *Anything.* She knew she could rely on me." She fell silent, and her gaze turned inward. Confronting the memory of a deathbed promise, perhaps?

My mind shied away from that one. I thought about what Mary Ann's childhood must have been like. I saw her shut up in a parlor amid the massive furniture I had seen in her apartment, grinding away at the Steinway while her mother cracked the whip or the silver cord or whatever. Who knew better than I what a wonderful time-consumer dull, slogging routine could be? The hours routine didn't fill I could imagine just as easily. I could see that pinch-faced, embittered woman seated in the garnet plush armchair, pouring out her grievances to her all-too-attentive daughter—grievances all the heavier because never in this life would she be able to have the last word with the person she wanted to have it with.

No wonder I had been haunted all night long by Blake's Poison Tree. My unconscious had been looking ahead to the future. Or was it back to the past and Korovskaya's Law?

When I speak of Korovskaya's Law, I mean the discourtesy title her students gave the philosophy she drummed into us as relentlessly as knee-over-the-toe, often following us out of the studio and haranguing as through the dressing room door in her hoarse, heavily accented English. The substance of it was that *amour-propre* is the source of harmony and more or less makes the world go round; one tampers with it at one's peril. We thought she had a bee in her bonnet and most of the time had all we could do not to giggle, though I recall one impassioned, graphic disquisition on the connection between wounded pride and the Holocaust that made our hair stand on end.

The bee was out in the open and buzzing around like a dive-bomber. For if this wasn't a case of wounded pride corroding the soul and unleashing havoc on the world at large, what was it?

Mary Ann's attention was fixed on me again. I realized I was expected to say something. "Your mother must have been an extraordinary woman to have inspired such devotion." God, how inane it sounded.

But it seemed to serve. "Oh, she was. Truly. She was wonderful." Mary Ann's face lit up. "She said I look exactly like she used to look when she was younger. Do you think so?"

I nodded, not trusting myself to speak. I didn't remember what her mother looked like. Hardly surprising, since I'd seen her only twice. The first time, at the garden party where the *Pas de Quatre* had made such a show of vamping her husband, I had confined myself to the occasional glance to see how the act was going over. The second time, at the short service arranged by Terry's friends before his body was shipped west, she had worn a veil.

Little Mrs. Woebegone, Nina had called her. Mousy had been my appraisal of her at the time. I remembered that Tagliaferro had referred to Mary Ann as "the mouse." Like mother, like daughter.

The very last thing anybody would expect was that either one might be dangerous. Scratch hard enough, though, and practically any living creature can turn dangerous. For Mary Ann's mother, having her husband stolen away had given her ample cause to hate the thieves; when he took his life, she must have blamed us for that, too. Easy to understand how she had longed for revenge, poured that longing into her daughter's ear drop by poisoned drop. Was it any wonder she had created a monster?

My mind balked at "monster." Looking at Mary Ann, I saw the same waif I had always seen. The glitter in her eyes, which I wanted in the worst way to interpret as dementia, looked like a touch of overexcitement. Well, if I had trouble crediting "monster," I should certainly be able to credit "murderess." Except that it was a B-movie word fraught with B-movie menace, and Woman's Lib ridicule of the suffix hadn't helped it any. Trying to affix these lurid labels to Mary Ann made my head reel, as if I had stepped through a cracked looking glass.

Yet she had killed three people, and I was next on her agenda. Fact, not fantasy. The gun in that competent right hand was steady as could be.

I thought about how I had instinctively recoiled from this girl and how my sense of fair play had taken me to task for it. From here on out I would never doubt my gut feelings again.

From here on out. What irony.

"The wheels are really turning, aren't they?" Mary Ann was smiling the tight little smile again. My efforts to sort things out mentally seemed to please her. Why? Did she feel a need to justify herself? To brag about how clever she'd been? Or simply to let somebody else know what it was all about? With the others there could scarcely have been opportunity for explanations.

Why didn't really matter. The important thing was to keep her talking, force myself to listen without showing any of the revulsion I felt. As long as she was talking, she wouldn't be shooting. Simple as that.

"Yes, they're turning," I said. "A matter of an eye for an eye. I can understand that. But surely four eyes for one is a bit excessive." I bit my lip, remembering that my mother once prophesied that I would crack wise on my deathbed.

"It wasn't excessive. Not a bit. Mother was worth ten of the lot of you. No, a *hundred*. God made her warm, loving, caring. That was the way she started out, the way she would have been all her life if it hadn't been for you. You had to come along and destroy that warmth, trample it into the ground. She never stopped grieving over what you did to her, she never stopped suffering. *Never.*"

Her mother. Only her mother. Why didn't she have a single thing to say about her father? Had his weakness in succumbing to our blandishments constituted a sin beyond redemption, turned him into a nonperson, like a member of an orthodox Jewish family who marries a gentile?

Useless to speculate. I had to talk so she would go on talking, watch for a moment when she let down her guard.

And then?

Don't think. Talk.

"It must have been a great comfort to your mother to know you intended to devote yourself to—" My tongue faltered. Revenge? Vengeance? Vendetta? Operatic, whatever the choice, yet mot juste all the same. "I mean, I assume she knew what you intended to do. Was it—Was it something she asked you to do?"

"Not in so many words, no. But I knew she wanted it. After all, she'd told me often enough that if it hadn't been for me she would have devoted her life to getting even. When she was dying—she had cancer, it took her a long time to die—I used to tell her over and over again I would get even for her. She liked hearing me say it. She knew I would be as good as my word."

My stomach churned. It was even worse than the deathbed pledge I had shied off imagining. I fervently hoped my face didn't show what I felt.

"After she died I sold the house and came east. I found *you* right away—all I had to do was open a phone book. And once I'd made contact with you it was easy to locate the others."

Made contact. Infiltrated the enemy camp, which hadn't been alerted to the danger of fallout from trivial pursuits of yesteryear. Locating the others must have been easy indeed, as easy as walking up the stairs when I was busy in the studio and looking in the address book on the shelf under the telephone.

"It all went so well I got a bit overconfident and formed a rather grandiose plan that involved warning each of you before I punished you. Fortunately, I realized how silly that would be—four of you and only one of me—and I changed my plan before I went too far with it."

Not, however, before sending a trashed poster of the *Pas de Quatre* to Nina, who was bothered enough to pump Donnie about possible long-lived animosities, but not bothered enough to be on her guard.

"You seem to have been very efficient. It was clever of you to make the first strike at a distance so no alarms would go off for the rest of us. And to choose the easiest target—an ordinary housewife who probably never even suspected the car that hit her was deliberately trying to. Not that pushing a spaced-out junkie out the window would have been much more of a challenge. I expect Nina was a far tougher proposition."

"Actually, she wasn't. I scouted her very carefully, you see. I counted on her arriving for the party alone and a bit late, so she could make an entrance. I waited in here till I saw her get out of the taxi. Then I met her on the landing and asked her if I could talk to her privately for a minute, it was very important. She wasn't best pleased, but she said okay, if I promised to make it quick. It was quick. She hardly had a chance to be surprised, much less frightened."

I remembered how Nina had looked when I walked in and found her lying here. Death, then, had been as sudden as appearances indicated. A small mercy.

"What would you have done if she'd met other guests at the door? Lured her away from the party?"

"Oh no, that would have been too risky. I had an alternative plan to resort to, if I had to. I would have arranged for her to go upstairs on another occasion, thinking you were expecting her. I wish now I did have to resort to it. Then you wouldn't still be walking around scot-free. You've been unbelievably lucky."

Lucky? Me? Under other circumstances that would have been

funny, considering how long I had wallowed in that bog of self-pity. Even after pulling out of it, I had continued to see my lot as more or less wobbling through my days.

I suddenly realized that I wanted very much to go on wobbling.

"I suppose I have been lucky."

"Of course you have. You were the perfect suspect. *Your* studio. *Your* skewer. Nina's jewelry hidden in *your* bathroom. What was it but luck that you found it before the police did? They were supposed to assume you'd had another quarrel. It was a good plan. It should have worked. It *would* have worked if the police hadn't been so inept. They should have searched every inch of this building right away. *Every inch.*" Her voice vibrated with the kind of indignation you hear in the voices of people complaining of no-show sanitation men and maids who fail to dust on top of the mantel.

I practically had to bite my tongue to keep from offering the sarcastic commiseration that particular tone invariably elicits from me. Evidently my mother was right about my propensity to crack wise.

"Perhaps your plan was a little too elaborate. After all, you had to count on the efficiency of the municipal judiciary system as well as the police. Any one of a million things could have gone wrong."

"You don't understand. Actually, it couldn't have been simpler." The tight little smile appeared again. "Some aspects of the judiciary system are entirely predictable. If the police had arrested you, well, you're a solid citizen, aren't you? Solid citizens are able to post bail, so they wouldn't have locked you up and thrown away the key. You would have been free until the case came to trial. Only there wouldn't have been a trial. You wouldn't have been able to face it, you would have decided to end it all instead. Nobody would have wondered a bit."

"It sounds simple all right. And a little sadistic. At any rate,

I seem to have been singled out to suffer more than the others. But maybe the devil you know is easier to hate."

"That's not the way it was at all. I didn't single you out for anything. Penetrating your space might have been easy, but somehow that made getting at you hard, much harder than I thought it would be. The one time I had a real opportunity, that policeman barged in and ruined it. After that you were too much on your guard. Setting that car on fire was the only way. I didn't do it to make you suffer, but if you have suffered, well, it's not a patch on what you made Mother suffer, is it?"

"I suppose not." Once again I longed to blurt out the truth: the need for self-justification runs deep. Foolish. Downright idiotic. The idea was to keep her talking, not provoke her into making the quick, clean job of me she had made of the others.

I took a deep breath. "Don't you think it's possible that deep down you wanted to drag things out for me so I would understand what was happening to me and why it was happening?" The little speech sounded cheap and hollow, like the psychobabble it was.

"You mean revenge isn't as sweet if nobody knows about it?" Mary Ann's tone was scornful. "That's childish. The only thing that matters to me is that Mother should know what I've done, and I believe that wherever she is she does know. Justice might be imperfect in this world, but it's different in the next. I'm certain she's in a good place, watching me and rejoicing. I realize it's a place I'm unlikely to go with blood on my hands, in case you're wondering. I've thought about it a lot, and I intend to devote the rest of my life to penance. I know it won't be easy to make my peace with God. Maybe I'll never be able to. So be it."

There was a fierce glint in her eye that looked like—what? Lunacy was too easy. More like the kind of light Hollywood has made a commonplace in the eyes of those prepared to give their all for a cause, from Joan of Arc and John Brown down to your garden variety terrorist. Whatever faint hope I had that I might be able to talk her out of killing me I lost right then.

But I had to keep trying. "You realize that if you shoot me now you'll probably have to do your penance in a cell. Nobody's going to believe it's suicide."

"Nobody's supposed to. How could they when the police didn't do their job? I abandoned that idea long ago."

Of course she had. The burning chariot was meant to look like an accident. And needless to say suicides don't mail out announcements of their demise or send themselves wreaths.

"Somebody might hear the shot. If one of my afternoon students should happen to get here early for a warm-up—"

"It wouldn't do you a bit of good. You locked the door, remember?" Mary Ann took a step toward me.

I backed away.

"Stand still! It will be less painful that way, I assure you. The closer I am, the better the chance I'll hit exactly what I aim at."

I stopped moving, wondering if she meant to put the bullet into my head or into my heart, wondering if the pain would be more intense at point-blank range. I watched her advance. Slowly, but not slowly enough. One more step and she would be within kicking distance.

My heart gave a flutter. I know to a fare-thee-well what kicking distance is; I've known it since the day I worked too close to another dancer at the barre and accidentally kicked her butt and had her turn on me with flailing fists.

Mary Ann took another step.

"Please." I made a stop sign with my hands. "Give me a moment or two. I'd like to collect my thoughts."

She pursed her lips, and the glass-fronted stare bored into me. I thought she was going to refuse, but instead she gave me a condescending nod. "You're not a hypocrite, I'll give you that. I thought you were going to say you wanted to pray, which I wouldn't have believed for a second. You have two minutes."

Even if I had been inclined toward prayer, I would have known better than to say so, for fear she might blow me away instantly and never mind getting close enough for a good shot: she wouldn't have wanted her God to entertain a last minute plea for forgiveness from the likes of me.

"Thank you." I bowed my head and concentrated on willing my body to perform what it hadn't performed in more than two decades.

In grand battement, the working leg flashes upward, cutting the air like a sword. To do it right, you need practice and proper warm-up.

Above all, you need a strong supporting leg. Which was precisely what I lacked.

I raised my head, saw something flicker in Mary Ann's eyes. Suspicion? Was she tuning in on my thought processes?

Now or never. I thrust up my right leg, and my pointed toe, hard as steel, caught her under the chin with a sharp crack. Her head jerked backward. She dropped to the floor. The gun flew out of her hand and skimmed across the floorboards and came to rest under the piano, quite some distance away. Not that distance counted for anything now. I knew she was dead. I knew I had broken her neck. The knowledge failed to kindle any feeling in me. Not regret, not relief, not anything. My brain recorded the information, that was all.

I shuddered, suddenly realizing that Mary Ann, spread-eagled on her back at my feet, was lying just about where Nina had been lying when I found her. Perhaps on the exact same spot. Perhaps things do come full circle. All traces of the police chalk outline were long gone, of course, so I would never know for sure.

Once before, an eternity ago, I had to force myself to scrutinize a body, and it was the same now. Mary Ann's face was a blank sheet of paper, just as Nina's had been. But the eyes behind the glasses (astonishingly, still in place) were closed. Whatever I had seen in them at the last—or imagined I had seen in them—was hidden from me now.

Mary Ann's sprawl was ungainly; Nina had looked graceful even in death. My brain registered that as a positive, and not only because the idea of perfect symmetry would have been hideous to contemplate. The difference seemed to provide objective evidence that Nina was better than Mary Ann.

Appalling to be making such a comparison, rating the woman I had killed as if the worth of the victim could possibly make the slightest bit of difference. I should have been disgusted with myself. I wasn't. Mary Ann was the one who had established the rating system: "Mother was worth ten of the lot of you. No, a *hundred*." Not true, Mary Ann. Just plain not true.

I forced myself to stare at the dead, unsurprised face. In a moment I would start to feel something. You don't kill another human being and not feel anything at all. Even if she is somebody who has killed three people and done her damnedest to kill you.

What had Mary Ann felt when she ran down Karin? When she pushed Allie out of the window? When she stabbed Nina? To hear her tell it, nothing: she had been exacting justice, like a hangman. But I didn't believe that. I had seen the exaltation she hadn't quite been able to mask—the same exaltation that Stu Cottman had interpreted as a sexual signal at the party and responded to accordingly.

One thing I could say for myself, I wasn't feeling any sense of triumph. Which put me way up over Mary Ann, didn't it?

There I went with the scales again. Stupid, stupid, stupid. As if anything mattered at this point except that Mary Ann was dead and I had killed her.

My stomach heaved mightily, warning me that I was about to be sick.

Oh no, I wasn't. I couldn't be sick. Not yet. I had to get myself up those stairs. Pick up the phone. Call the police.

Something clicked in my head. I could hear Sergeant Tagliaferro's voice again, calling Mary Ann "the mouse."

Like mother, like daughter.

How like is like?

All at once, my memory went into overdrive. I recalled how Terry Sablier's suicide had stunned practically everybody who knew him. Not only because it had been so unexpected, but because it had seemed inconceivable that Terry, a devotee of homeopathic medicine who wouldn't even touch aspirin, should have polluted his body with barbiturates. Where he got the sleeping pills nobody ever knew, but of course when you're desperate you find a way. And Donnie had been quick to bare his breast and shout "Mea culpa," which pretty much squelched everybody's doubts.

My doubts, dormant all these years, were revitalized. I was imagining another scenario. I was imagining Little Mrs. Woebegone, discarded and feeling wronged beyond endurance, taking measures to turn herself into a widow with the same self-righteous ruthlessness she had passed on to her daughter. And there might well have been an additional motive. At least half of every check Terry ever received went into his bank account, which, considering his earning capacity, must have been substantial. Wasn't it possible that the prospect of returning to Oak Grove and starting life anew as comfortably fixed widow rather than as abandoned wife had provided sufficient incentive for murder? That things had subsequently gone wrong, whether because word of the failed marriage had got about, as Mary Ann believed, or because being the relict of a suicide carried another kind of stigma? Or maybe there hadn't been any stigma. Maybe guilt feelings had festered and caused the transference of blame to what she perceived as the source of all her troubles—the *Pas de Quatre*. Admittedly, it was a scenario heavily weighted with pop psychology, but none the less believable for that.

Still, only a scenario. No part of it was verifiable. No part of it would ever be verifiable. Just as well, very likely. What good would it do Donnie to find out that two decades of self-flagellation were all for nothing?

What good would it do anybody, all things considered, to find out that the total of people wantonly slaughtered was four instead of three? No, five. I was forgetting my own contribution.

Better not to think about that until I had to. That I would have to I didn't doubt for a moment. I had just killed somebody.

Down the road—not very far down the road—I would have to pay for it, even if the law didn't exact a penalty.

I walked out of the studio without looking back and started up the stairs to telephone the police. The scent of lilies came with me every step of the way.